DECEPTION

JANE FLAGELLO

ZIG ZAG PRESS LLC

ISBN-13: 978-0-9961237-9-2

Editing by Demon for Details
Cover design by WickedSmartDesigns.com
Interior formatting by Author E.M.S.

Zig Zag Press LLC
Virginia Beach, VA
2018

Published in the United States of America

OTHER BOOKS BY JANE FLAGELLO

Fiction

Bamboozled

Gotcha!

Complicity

Mercy

Non-Fiction

The Change Intelligence Factor: Mastering the Promise of Extra-Ordinary

CHAPTER 1

"Doin' the best I can for her. Not like I got choices. Don' got no insurance." Mrs. Lee's chin wobbled while she blinked hard against tears.

"I appreciate how much you love your daughter," said Dr. McKenna, slowly breathing past the ache in her heart for yet another sick child.

The ER had been crazy these past few nights, overwhelmed with sick children, the hardest patients for Debra McKenna to treat because their pain tugged at her heart. Debra's mind blipped briefly to her day off tomorrow. Hearing her name called, and feeling her cell phone vibrating on her hip, brought her back to the here and now in the swamped ER.

She looked at the distraught woman standing next to her and then at Detective Knight, who had positioned himself to the woman's right, allowing McKenna to lead the conversation while he observed.

"Right now we need your help, Mrs. Lee. Detective Knight and I need your help. Lette needs your help."

Mrs. Lee looked at the little girl and gently caressed her hand. The suddenness of the touch caused Lette to pull her hand away. "We was gettin' it from the clinic. We'd take the bus up and Miss Amiee would check Lette over an' give it to me. But it shut down last month." Tear-filled eyes turned to Knight. "I didn' know what else to do. When this man tol' me about the flea market, I... I... I had to check it out."

"I understand." Knight nodded while scribbling on his notepad.

"Somethin's better than nothin'. So I paid him thirty dollas and he gave me the insulin. And he threw in the needles for free."

"And you only saw him that one time?" asked Knight.

"Yessir. Last week it was." Mrs. Lee stared at the floor. "I don' give her the full amount each time. Gotta make it last."

"Do you have any more of the insulin you bought from the man?" asked Dr. McKenna.

"Yes, ma'am," said Mrs. Lee. "I got me two bottles. He was running a BOGO. But I don' have any with me. Didn' think to bring it. With all the excitement."

"No worries. As long as there's more. I'd like to run some tests on it. Since you came by ambulance, I'll ask the driver who takes you home to bring back one of the vials."

"Oh, don' go to no trouble. We can call a taxi or somethin'."

"It will be our pleasure to take you both home in one of the hospital's vans."

"Thank you kindly. It's home in the 'frigerator, where Dr. Samuels tol' me to keep it."

"That's great." McKenna made a mental note to check on Dr. Samuels, since the name was unfamiliar to her.

"And where did you see Dr. Samuels?"

"At the Centerville clinic. He said he'd be in touch when he got to a new place, but I ain't heard from him." Mrs. Lee picked at a thread on her blouse. "So sad when the clinic closed."

"I'm sure it was," said Dr. McKenna. "Had you been going there long?"

"A coupla months. Since Lette took sick. Such a kind man, Dr. Samuels was. He showed me how t'use the insulin, what them numbers on the needles meant, an' how t'get air out of the needle, which he said was very important."

"Good to know."

"Bless my heart," said Mrs. Lee, touching her hand to her chest, "I used t'shake so in the beginnin'. Thought I'd drop the needle every time. But I practiced with an orange like he showed me. Lette be practicin' too. She's gettin' really good, so it won't be long before she'll be able to take care of herself."

"Does the man at the flea market who sold you the insulin have a name?" Knight asked.

"Sure he does, but I don' know it."

"Can you tell me anything about what he looked like? Short? Tall? Heavy? Thin? White? Black? Asian?"

"He was kinda heavy. Had trouble gettin' off his chair and was sweatin' like crazy. He wasn't a brother."

"So, a heavyset white guy?"

"Yessir. Dark hair. One of them mustaches 'at come down the sides of ya mouth." She moved her fingers along the sides of her own mouth.

"Would you recognize him if you saw him again?"

"Mebbe."

"If I brought in a sketch artist, do you think you could describe him?"

"I don' know." Tears left tracks down Mrs. Lee's cheeks. "What have I done? Did I hurt my little Lette?" Distressed eyes looked from Dr. McKenna to Detective Knight. "I jus' want Lette to feel better. And I didn' know what else to do." She touched the little girl's forehead. "Can you help her?"

3

"Of course," said Dr. McKenna. "We're getting her stabilized right now, and we'll monitor her progress for a few hours. Then we'll send you home with a supply of the medicine she needs."

"Thank you." Mrs. Lee pulled a tissue out of the box beside the bed and wiped her eyes.

"I'll also give you the name of someone from the hospital's outpatient clinic who can help you with Lette's insulin supplies, to help you make sure she gets what she needs and doesn't get sick again."

"I...I..." Mrs. Lee looked out the window. Barely above a whisper she said, "I don' make much money cleanin' the motel rooms where I work, and they don' have no health plan. I'm not sure I can pay—"

"Not something you need to worry about right now, Mrs. Lee." Dr. McKenna smiled warmly. "Let me get things moving along."

Dr. McKenna put a comforting hand on Mrs. Lee's arm and guided her to the chair. "You sit and try to relax. Can I call anyone for you?"

"No, ma'am. It's jes us. Family's back in Arkansas. Lette and me, we came up here to visit last year, an' she loved it so much. I never seen her so happy. Didn' have much back home, so we decided t'stay. I got me a job, and Lette started school. Everythin' was going so good, until she got sick. Then...then..." Tears swelled in Mrs. Lee's eyes and she turned away.

"Can I get you anything? Coffee? Tea?"

"No, thank you kindly. I be fine. You go on about yer business. You spent so much time with us already."

Debra smiled at this kindhearted woman. "I'll be back in a bit to check on you."

Dr. McKenna headed for the door. "Detective? Can I speak to you privately?"

"Here's my card, Mrs. Lee," said Knight. "I'll be in touch about the sketch artist. And if you remember anything else, please call me." He pulled out his cell while he walked out of the room.

Debra put her iPad down on the nurse's station counter and waited for Detective Knight to end his call.

"Thanks for coming."

"No problem. You okay?"

"I'm fine."

"If you're fine, I'm the Queen of England and we both know that ain't true."

Debra shook her head "We had a lot of injured kids tonight. Somehow an adult with a gunshot wound is easier to handle than a kid with a broken leg, or someone like Lette. And she's not the first."

"What do you mean?"

"She's my second child in as many days with insulin issues. And before I called you, I called over to Riverside. The ER doctor there told me they had two cases last week involving insulin. One parent played dumb, but the other parent said she got her insulin from a clinic on Centerville Road, just like Mrs. Lee."

"But Mrs. Lee finally admitted that she got her insulin from a guy at the flea market."

"I know. And according to the doctor at Riverside, his patient's parent also finally admitted the same thing. And he said it took a lot of hand-holding and making nice to get it out in the open."

"I'm worried about you."

"Don't worry. I'll be okay."

"Excuse me." Adam looked at the caller ID on his buzzing phone while he moved away. She saw his smile brighten when he came back.

"I called in a favor. Arturo, our best sketch artist, is on his way. He's really good at getting people to open up and remember details."

"Great. I'll call our public health advocate and get her working on Lette's case. She'll pull the right strings at our pharmacy to get a supply of the insulin Lette needs. Think I'll suggest she try to get Mrs. Lee to use auto-injectors. When she said she got free needles with the insulin, I cringed."

"How come?"

"First because they may not be sterile. And second because you've got to pull the right amount of insulin into the syringe. Too much or too little could do a lot of damage. The auto-injectors are the best invention since sliced bread."

"Sliced bread?" Knight checked his watch. "I'm hungry. Got time for coffee and a bagel? I missed breakfast."

"Not today. And sorry about getting you up so early. I needed you to meet Mrs. Lee and hear her story before she disappeared on me."

"That happens?"

Debra didn't immediately answer. Then, with a huge sigh, she said, "Happens all the time. They come in, we treat them, and, when no one's watching, they disappear because they don't have the money to pay the bill." Debra made some notes on her iPad. "What did you make of her story?"

"Flea markets are notorious for selling all sorts of stuff, some of which conveniently fell off the back of a truck."

"Insulin needs to be refrigerated. I've passed the flea market on Richmond Road several times, and as far as I can tell, it's all outside. A cooler's great for a day at the beach, but using a cooler to store insulin doesn't cut it."

"Do you think that's what happened? Just a case of spoilage?"

"I don't know. That's why I want to get Lette's insulin tested." Debra yanked off the scrunchie that held her long auburn hair in a ponytail and scratched the back of her neck. "Buying insulin from some sweaty, nameless guy at the flea market instead of a reputable pharmacist raises all sorts of red flags for me."

"I'm assuming you took blood."

"Of course. It's protocol."

"When will the labs come back?"

"We should have preliminary results shortly." McKenna looked back at the room and then at Adam. "Are you familiar with the Centerville clinic she mentioned?"

"Can't say that I am. What are you thinking?"

"That I know most of the doctors who work the clinics in this area, and I've never heard of a Dr. Samuels."

"I can ask some of the patrol guys what they know." Adam looked at his watch again. "It's Saturday. My shift doesn't start until four. Think I'll take a ride up Richmond Road and check out the flea market. See what I can see. Then I'll swing back here and see if Mrs. Lee has made any progress with the sketch artist."

"Sounds good."

"We still on for tomorrow?"

"You bet. It's been a crazy few days, and a couple of hours spent kayaking on the reservoir and soaking in the fall colors will do us both a world of good. Then we can lounge on my deck and I'll even make you dinner."

Adam smiled. "Sounds good. I'll touch base with you when I get back."

Debra watched him leave. They'd been dating for a few glorious months and she couldn't be happier. They clicked, and helped each other find balance in spite of their stressful jobs.

CHAPTER 2

Jesse followed the horde of disembarking foreign arrivals passengers streaming towards customs like sheep to the slaughter.

He dreaded the wasted hours getting through customs. He was tired. He was dirty. *Long flight. All I want is to get to Morgan's and take a long, hot shower.*

He'd spent the past two months traversing sub-Saharan Africa, reporting on population upheaval, collateral damage and deaths from ongoing civil wars with his last stop in the Democratic Republic of the Congo.

Things were uglier than his wildest nightmares. Purposeful genocide was the only way to describe the thousands upon thousands of deaths, mostly women and children, from brutal fighting and people crammed in refugee camps and living in deplorable conditions. His goal as a reporter was to tug at the heartstrings of powerful Americans and Europeans, to get them to care about the crises thousands of miles away. Surely raising their awareness, getting average people to speak out against the human tragedy unfolding on the African continent, would help.

Can anything really help? Probably not, but these endless wars and the senseless killing have to stop.

8

Most people were caught up in their own day-to-day dramas, and the world's struggles were easy to tune out when putting food on your table, keeping your kids safe, and working hard ruled your life.

Antifa, domestic mass shootings, the recent measles epidemic, and instances of typhus and tuberculosis surfacing in the homeless tent colonies on the streets of Los Angeles offered a glimmer of hope, because people were realizing they could be one sneeze, one airplane ride, one evening out with family and friends, one trip to the movies or the mall away from potential disaster.

"Excuse me," Jesse said to the man who jostled him and knocked his backpack off his shoulder to the floor, a tall, well-dressed man with coal-colored skin, salt and pepper hair cut close to his head, and piercing hazel eyes.

"*Pardonne moi.* I have a plane to catch." The man's French-accented English surprised Jesse, as did his retrieval of the fallen backpack. "*Ici.* Here." He brushed off unseen dirt. "*Pas de mal.* No harm done."

"This backpack's been around the world several times over. Nothing short of a bomb can hurt it."

"How long do you think this will take?" the man asked, nodding toward the line of people in front of them.

"Your guess is as good as mine," said Jesse. "Three planes just landed. We all have places to go, but they're here," he pointed to the customs agents working the line, "for their eight-hour shift, regardless of how many people they process, so there's no incentive to move any faster than a lava flow."

"*Oui.* Truly." The man stepped back, his head swiveling in all directions.

"I think we were on the same plane," said Jesse. "The United flight from Kinshasa? I noticed you when I was walking around to keep my blood circulating."

"*Je suis désolé*. I am sorry. With so many people on the plane, I do not recall."

"I'm easy to miss," laughed Jesse. "Twenty-plus hour flights are hard on the body so I walk around the cabin a lot. My legs are thrilled to move."

"I am fortunate. My company allows us to fly first class."

"What line of work are you in?"

"Global consulting."

"Are you with the UN?" asked Jesse, pointing to the blue global logo on the man's attaché case.

"Excuse me. I think I see an associate."

Jesse watched him join another line, which was just as long as Jesse's. But there was no associate. He didn't speak to anyone.

Sara stood in a sea of boxes, bubble wrap, packing paper, and tape.

"Where did I get all this stuff?"

She knew the answer. Two marriages, one son, and her own severe hoarder complex. Thirty years ago she moved into her New Jersey home with her first husband, then secured it during a hard-fought divorce. She made Marv live there when they got married, claiming the therapist said Howie was too fragile after his father abandoned him to force him to leave the only home he'd ever known.

But now it was time for out-with-the-old-in-with-the-new. If her BFF Rachel could move to a new place and find love in the process, she could too. Maybe not the love part, but she was so over New Jersey. It was time for a change.

Her cell phone blasted the notes of Carol King's, *You've Got A Friend*.

"Hey, Rachel. What's up?"

"Just calling to see how you're doing."

"Packing sucked, but unpacking sucks more. I don't know where I'm going to put all my stuff."

"Tell me about it. When I moved to Williamsburg, I swore I'd never move again. That didn't last long."

"Yeah, but that hunky husband of yours and that gorgeous home you built together was totally worth another move."

"True. I did give Daniel a heads-up that I'm never moving again."

"Good for you. That'll work until it doesn't and you move."

"Don't you know it, girlfriend."

"I can see the smile on your face from here." Sara batted a wad of used packing tape into an empty box. "Want to come to New Jersey with me tomorrow? I have some papers to sign and my attorney is a Luddite."

"A what?"

"A Luddite. Someone who doesn't believe in technology."

"You're kidding."

"Wish I was. What can I say? He's old. I'm taking Amtrak because it seems planes don't fly from here Newark at a reasonable hour."

"Not living by a major airport is the big downside to Williamsburg. That and crappy shopping."

"A relaxing train ride will be a welcome change from the craziness of moving. At least I won't have to take off my shoes and get technologically strip-searched."

"Cute. Sure, I'll come along. I'll bring my mah jongg travel set and we can play Siamese on the way up and back."

"Great idea."

"Let's call Beth and Ellyn. Maybe we can get dinner and a game together."

"Sounds like fun. Chinese?"

"What else? Playing mah jongg requires eating Chinese."

"We can spend the night at Ellyn's and come back Monday."

"Which gives you a break from unpacking and both of us a chance to see Ellyn and Beth, get in lots of mah jongg and some good 'girl time.' And when we get back I can help you with your unpacking if you want me to."

"Thanks. I packed the Jersey house so fast, I'm finding more stuff I'll never use again. The ReStore is going to think it hit the lottery."

"I love that you bought my old house here."

"Your old house is not even five years old, and I loved it the moment you showed it to me right before you bought it."

"I loved that house too. Planned to live there until they carried me out. But—"

"But along came Daniel and everything changed."

"For the better."

"I'll drink to that." Sara's attention was drawn to the front door. "Gotta go. Someone's at the door. If I don't see you later, I'll see you tomorrow. Go online and buy your ticket. The train leaves at 7:30."

"Will do. Daniel will take us to the station. Pick you up at 6:45."

Sara peeked through the sidelight curtains, then flung open the door.

"Howie! What are you doing here?"

"Can't a guy visit his mother?"

"What kind of trouble are you in this time?" He brushed past her and dropped his duffel bag on the living room floor.

"Nice place. Gated community. Ritzy neighborhood. Better than Jersey." He found the kitchen and helped himself to a beer. Twisting off the cap, he leaned on the counter and guzzled half of it.

He smiled at her. "I'm not in any trouble."

"I've heard that line before." His insolent stare rattled her, but she'd promised herself to stick to her guns the next time Howie came calling. So she recited several past examples, her voice flat, her eyes not leaving his.

"Enough, Ma."

"I can continue. There's lots more."

"And you love reminding me, don't you?"

"Not really. But I need you to understand where I'm coming from. My house. My rules. Understand?"

"Understand. I don't know what you think I'm going to do, but I get the ground rules. I just need to crash for a few days."

"You can stay as long as you want…as long as you…"

"Obey your rules." He finished the beer. "I got it, Ma. I got it."

Soraya's plane landed on time, and she strode briskly through Dulles to ground transportation, where she identified herself to a uniformed chauffeur who had her name on a sign.

"Your baggage claim checks, please."

He collected her luggage and led the way to the silver blue Bentley Mulsanne, where a second uniformed man was waiting with the passenger door open. She slipped inside and turned down the blasting air conditioning.

"Hay-Adams please."

"Yes, ma'am."

She opened the drink cooler nestled between the two back seats and selected a bottle of Aqua Deco water. Her cell phone beeped and she looked at the caller ID.

"My flight just landed and I'm on my way to the Hay. Is everything secure on your end?"

"Yes, ma'am." The woman had a slight British accent. "Director Obi is expecting your visit."

"Does she know what I want to speak with her about?"

"No, ma'am. I've kept our previous conversation close to the vest. She'll be surprised. That is what you want, isn't it?"

"Yes, very much."

Soraya ended the call and settled back into the soft leather seat for the ride to DC. The next few days would determine her future…either retirement to a life of excessive luxury or needing to accept another contract. She was more than ready for the luxurious retirement option.

CHAPTER 3

Adam drove up Richmond Road and stopped at the New York deli for a Reuben. He would have preferred a bagel and coffee with Debra McKenna, but she was too busy for food. Hopefully tomorrow's weather would be a repeat of today, mid-eighties and not a cloud tarnishing the bright blue sky. Kayaking and grilling steaks with Debra was the best way he could think of to relax on a Sunday.

The Toano flea market was more like a traveling road show. Vendors came from all over, hawking a huge variety of new and used goods, and the parking lot of the shuttered strip mall was jam-packed when Adam pulled in. He flashed his badge, and was given a prime parking spot and comped the two-fifty entrance fee.

The market closed at two on Saturdays, and it was already noon, so he had a lot of ground to cover.

Mrs. Lee remembered the guy she bought the insulin from used a multicolored umbrella to shield him from the sun's rays. She said they'd talked about the heat and humidity for a good bit of time, and when he noticed Lette was getting uncomfortable, he offered her a bottle of water. That turned their conversation to diabetes, which was when he told her about the insulin he had for sale.

Adam adjusted his sunglasses and scanned the flea market, zeroing in on three multicolored umbrellas along the far left side of the lot.

Considering the time, he was glad they were close to each other. He ambled by the first booth but didn't see a cooler. The man running the booth was in deep conversation with the guy at the next booth about ice fishing in Minnesota.

The second booth looked more promising when he spied a red Coleman cooler tucked behind the vendor's high-back director's chair. He pulled out his cell and snapped a few photos of the guy, who also had a horseshoe moustache like the one Mrs. Lee described. He was reading the latest issue of Men's Health magazine. The guy's Suburban was parked behind the stall, and Adam roamed behind several booths to get a shot of the license plate.

"Nice afternoon," said Adam when he finally approached the vendor.

"Too hot for my blood." He pulled out a bandana and wiped the back of his neck. "What can I help you find?"

"Looking for vintage belt buckles. Been collecting the things since I was a kid. Actually found an old Confederate one from the Civil War a few weeks ago at a flea market in Richmond."

"Wouldn't mind finding something like that myself. Most of what I've got is pretty standard. Nothing that old. You might try Shorty's table." He pointed to the other side of the parking lot. "He sometimes comes up with some pretty cool stuff. Don't know where he gets it."

Adam pulled out a tissue and made a show of wiping his forehead. "Damn. This heat gets to me big time, and it's not even that hot today." He wiped around the back of his neck. "Just got diagnosed with Type 2 and my body's still getting used to my insulin injections."

"Know what you mean. Type 2's no fun. My sister's Type 2 and she's always fighting the heat." The guy slipped off his chair and opened the cooler. He pulled out a bottle of water and handed it to Adam. "On the house. I keep spares with me because you never know when you're gonna need water."

"Thanks." Adam twisted off the cap and took a huge gulp. "Mind if I grab a handful of ice to rub on the back of my neck? Feeling like I need to cool down fast."

"Not at all. Help yourself."

Adam dug his hand into the cooler, feeling for anything that might be a vial of insulin. Finding a vial in the cooler would be too good to be true, but no such luck. Regardless, the guy's familiarity with diabetes made him a definite person of interest.

"Thanks again." Adam rubbed the cubes against the back of his neck.

"If you can come back next week, I'll check with some friends to see if they have any interesting belt buckles for you to look at."

"That would be great." Adam took another gulp of water. "So, you're here every week?"

"Pretty much. I get here early so I can get this back row and park my truck next to me. Makes set up and tear down a lot easier than lugging the stuff from where they make vendors park."

"Makes sense." Adam finished off the water. "Don't go to no trouble, but I'll be sure to stop by next Saturday in case you happen to find any buckles. I also like gun manufacturers' logos."

"Come early," said the vendor, handing Adam a business card. "Never know when I'm gonna get a run on belt buckles."

"Randy Jackson," said Adam reading the guy's name from the card.

"That's me." He extended his hand.

"Nice to meet you. Bruce…Bruce Wayne."

"Batman! Bet you took your share of ribbing as a kid."

"Yeah. It's worn off finally. These days most people don't know Batman's real name. So shhhh. Don't tell." Adam turned to walk away, but said over his shoulder, "See you next Saturday."

It was well past four when Debra made it to the solitude of her tiny office. She had larger cubicles when she was a resident at Sloane Kettering in New York, but, tiny as it was, this was her private space, a refuge from the life and death dramas taking place all around her.

She leaned back in her chair, tapped her iPhone, got into her photos, and scrolled to the one she wanted. All it took to restore her soul was a few minutes alone gazing at the very handsome face of Detective Adam Knight. Adam was sitting in a yellow kayak in the middle of the reservoir behind her house, the setting sun framing him in a subtle pink glow.

She closed her eyes and remembered the day. It was their second date, a week after their dinner at Giuseppe's. The meal had been good, his company better.

A rush of heat overwhelmed her. Too many years had passed without so much as a boyfriend. Her medical training had consumed her, but now she had the time, the inclination, and she was gazing at the face of an interesting possibility.

They hadn't ventured far into the physical aspects of their relationship. Yet. The timing hadn't been right. She licked her lips. Maybe tomorrow, after kayaking the afternoon away, after a good steak dinner and a nice bottle of wine, things would lend themselves to a more intimate exploration.

"Knock-knock." Burt, the driver who took Mrs. Lee and Lette home, stood at her office door. "Sorry to disturb you, but I thought you'd want this." He handed her a small vial.

"Thanks, Burt. I hope it wasn't too much trouble to drive them home. I didn't want them to take a taxi, and I really need this." She held up the insulin vial.

"No problem. A sweet lady, and Lette, she's smart as a whip."

"Where do they live?"

"Way over on the other side of town. The Grove. I'm surprised the ambulance didn't take them to Riverside. It was closer."

"Its ER was handling the truck accident victims from Route 64 this morning, so it was overwhelmed." Debra fingered the vial. "Tell me about their house. Did you manage to get a peek inside like I asked?"

"Yep. It's not much from the outside. Kind of run-down, and a few cans of paint would definitely help. But the inside was immaculate. Nicely furnished, with everything in its place. Even got to see Lette's room because she wanted to show me her seashell collection."

"And?"

"A pink wonderland. Reminded me of pictures in the books I read to my grandkids. Cinderella's castle in pink and white."

Debra felt her smile. "Good to know."

"There was one thing that surprised me."

"What's that?"

"No pictures. There weren't any photos of Lette and her mom or other family. My house is full of photos. You can't look anyplace and not see one of my kids or grandkids framed for posterity."

"Curious, but maybe Mrs. Lee keeps her photos on her phone and doesn't print any out."

19

"That could be, but since you asked me to look around, I thought that was interesting." Burt pointed to the vial. "Do you want me to drop that off at the lab? I'm heading that way to pick up Cindy Lou from daycare."

"No. I'll take it down. My car's parked out that way."

"Lucky us having tomorrow off. See you Monday."

Debra was happy to see Jasmine's smiling face when she opened the door to the lab on her way out. All the techs were good, but Jasmine added something extra special to her work. She took the time to be thorough.

"Thanks for waiting for me," said Debra when she opened the door.

"No problem, girl. What have you got for me?"

"Insulin vial. Had a little girl come in this morning with a very bad reaction to whatever is in this vial."

"That's not good."

Debra handed the vial to Jasmine, who filled out the label on a small plastic bag and dropped in the vial.

"I'm here all night, and I've just got this one set of labs to finish up, so I can start on this pretty soon. Unless, of course, all hell breaks loose. It is Saturday night, plus there's a full moon."

"Don't remind me. Glad I'm out of here for twenty-four hours."

"Got anything interesting planned? And don't tell me no, because I saw that hunky detective leave the ER when I was coming into work. The way he looks at you. Kind of like my kids looking at a hot fudge sundae they can't wait to devour."

Debra laughed. "Adam is coming over tomorrow for some R & R. We both need to chill."

"Sounds good to me. I wouldn't mind chilling with him lying next to me."

"Jasmine, the man you're married to is no slouch. He did make the cover of GQ a few years ago."

"He won a contest." Her eyes went to a magazine cover photo sitting in a silver frame on her desk. "And he does look hot on that cover."

"And the two of you have made two beautiful children."

"Don't I know it. Smart, too. Did I tell you Olivia got a full scholarship to Princeton? Her SAT score was off the charts, so even though she's only a junior, they made her an offer."

"And she accepted?"

"On the spot. She wants to be a doctor, an ER doctor like you. It's all she talks about."

"That's great. You tell her to come see me if she has questions or needs any help. Bet I can wangle her a summer job next year doing small stuff around the ER so she can get a feel for what it's like."

"That would be awesome. I'll get these results to you as soon as I can."

"See you Monday."

"Have fun. Don't do anything I wouldn't do…which gives you tons of leeway to have one heck of a good time."

CHAPTER 4

"You've had a long day. Penny for your thoughts," said Morgan as she joined Jesse on the deck and handed him a glass of wine.

"Everyone thinks international travel is so glamorous. Actually, it's a pain in the ass." He held up his wine glass to hers. "Cheers. It's good to be home."

"Makes my welcome-home dinner all the more special."

Jesse'd been gone for two months on a freelance assignment in Africa. The political climate was a mess, mostly corrupt politicians fighting for power. Jesse's boss wanted dirt on anything UN-related so he could advance his personal agenda to further discredit what he believed to be a corrupt, useless international organization. Jesse was in total agreement and eagerly accepted the assignment.

"Interesting thing happened when I was going through customs at Dulles."

"Interesting things are always happening to you." Morgan turned on the grill, then pulled a cushion out of the storage chest, put it on the chair next to him, and sat down. "The steaks won't take long once the grill gets hot. We've got about ten minutes until I put the potatoes on. So tell me, what was so interesting?"

"Met this very distinguished-looking man going through customs. He literally bumped into me while I was in the customs line. Considering how tired I was, I'm surprised I didn't land on my ass."

"Must have been some bump."

"It was. He apologized. We chatted briefly, then he excused himself to join a friend."

"Seems normal to me. What made it interesting?"

"He lied. There was no friend. I watched him. He just went to another line, but didn't talk to anyone."

"Maybe he wanted to get away from you."

"What? Why? I'm adorable."

"Yes, you are. To me. Others have described you as a pain in the ass, contentious, threatening, pugnacious, an out-of-control renegade, and a loose cannon."

"All endearing qualities, if you ask me."

"No one is asking you." Morgan sipped her wine and looked at Jesse. "Let me get this straight. A guy bumps you, you almost fall on your ass, you chat, and he walks away. That's it?"

"Yeah. He knocked my backpack off my shoulder and actually picked it up, brushed it off, and handed it back to me."

"That's just being polite. Shows good upbringing."

"But he lied. When there was no need to."

"Maybe he was embarrassed about bumping into you. And you immediately think there's something sinister about it."

"Occupational hazard."

"What?"

"Not believing what people tell you. People lie."

"Not all people lie."

"That's not been my experience." Jesse finished his wine and refilled both their glasses. "I saw him later in the parking garage getting into a black SUV. A second lie, and to me, a perfect stranger, about having to catch another flight. Why?"

"Maybe it was his way of excusing himself without seeming rude."

"That could be." Jesse stared out into space. "Dulles is huge. What are the odds his ride and my car would be in the same garage area?"

"That is a little weird."

"There was something—"

"You think about the something while I get the potatoes." Morgan got up and headed into the house. "I'll open another bottle of wine. Can't expect you to cook without a beverage."

"Sounds good to me."

They ate on the deck and were finishing the second bottle of wine when Jesse said, "While I was looking into how the refugees were faring in one of the camps, this little boy latched onto me. He was the cutest kid. Big brown eyes. The kind of smile that lights up a room. He told me his name was Marcel. One afternoon he took my hand and led me to a field where his friends had started a pickup soccer game. He was quite good and everyone was laughing and having fun…until the explosion. One of the kids tripped a land mine."

"Oh! Was he hurt?"

"Several kids were hurt, Marcel included. The medical team rushed to the field, and I remember carrying Marcel to the makeshift hospital. He smiled all the way. Brave kid. He wound up with a broken leg and some superficial scratches which the doctors treated with antibiotics. No parents showed up, so I stayed with him that night so he wouldn't be afraid. He had surgery to set his leg, and I kept him company playing Go Fish. He killed me every game, but I could tell something was wrong. He was in a lot of pain. And then he developed an infection."

"That's not good. What kind of infection?"

"Never heard a name, but I'm sure it was something easily treated with antibiotics. And they were giving him antibiotics, orally at first, but when the infection didn't resolve itself and his fever spiked, the doctors started an IV."

Jesse looked away so Morgan wouldn't see the tears in his eyes.

"I overheard one of the doctors tell the nurse to get the special drug. She gave him a funny look, and he yelled 'Do it.' I hung around in the hall, pretending to read a magazine, but my attention was glued to the curtain, waiting for the nurse to return. She was gone about fifteen minutes and came back with several vials in her hand."

"What was the special drug?"

"I don't know." Jesse got up. "Be right back."

When he came back he had two vials in his hand. "This is the IV drug Marcel was getting," he said holding up the vial with a silver cap. "And this one with the red cap is the one the nurse brought back, the special drug."

"What are they?"

"I don't know." Jesse laid the two vials on the table and sat back down on the chaise. "Marcel looked like he was responding to the special drug." Jesse bowed his head and dug his fingers into his eyes. "But it was too late. He died."

"I'm so sorry." Morgan leaned over and touched his arm.

"The nurse was furious. I saw her follow the doctor into a supply area, so I stood by the curtain to see if I could hear their conversation while I started the record app on my iPhone. My French is passable, and I kept hearing her scream *stupide*."

"Not hard to translate that."

"She was screaming about how stupid the doctor's decision was, how he'd wasted the good drug on the boy when he knew it was already too late."

25

"The 'good drug?'"

"I'm sure that's what she said. *La bonne drogue.*" Jesse picked up the two vials, one in each hand and looked at Morgan. "Good drug…bad drug?"

"What's the actual drug?" Morgan took one of the vials. "This label is all numbers. Must be a code."

"Don't know, but I'm going to find out."

"How?"

"Calling in a favor from a friend who works at the lab at Johns Hopkins. I'll drive these up to Baltimore so he can test them and tell me what they are."

"Great idea." Morgan finished her wine. "You said you recorded the doctor and nurse?"

"Yeah, but it's hard to understand everything they're saying. It's in French and they're talking really fast."

"I've got friends too. And one works at the local radio station. I'll bet they have some high-tech equipment that might be able to capture a clearer copy of what's on your phone."

"But it's in French."

"Excuse me? William & Mary? Big college? I'm sure someone there speaks French and can help us."

"Ain't it great to have friends."

Morgan leaned back into the chaise's cushions and thought for a few moments. "Does anyone know you have these?"

"I didn't think so. No one was around when I snatched them, and with all the chaos, I don't think they have the same drug security protocols in these makeshift hospitals as we do in hospitals here, but now I'm not so sure."

"The guy at the airport?"

"Yeah. I think I'm being followed."

"By who?"

"More of a what. A black SUV."

"The one from the airport?"

"Don't know. Could be. I've seen it a few times since I got back from the Congo."

"Black SUV? There are hundreds of black SUVs on the road."

"I know. But airport guy got into one, and then I noticed one behind me coming out of Dulles.

"Correct me if I'm wrong, but there is only one way out of Dulles, so anyone leaving the airport would of necessity have to be behind you, beside you or in front of you."

Jesse sighed. "True, but that same vehicle was somewhere near me all the way down 95."

"How do you know it was the same SUV?"

"DC plates. SAA 0456." Jesse finished his wine and stood up. "I snapped a photo." He held up his cell for her to see the image.

"Could you see who was driving?"

"No. Tinted windows. Every time I got close enough to almost see the driver, it sped up."

"So then he may not have been following you. It could have been your overly active and suspicious imagination."

"No. Because a few miles later, there it was again. There wasn't much traffic, so it had to have slowed down. Why would someone be following me?"

"Good question. Guess you need someone to run the plates?"

"Yep." He held his hand over the grill to make sure it was cool enough to close the cover. "Think your FBI-connected uncle might be willing?"

"Won't know until you ask him."

"He barely knows me. I'm water, you're blood, and blood's thicker than water."

"Blood that's once, twice, three times removed."

"He's helped you before. When Nadine Green was killed.

And you've gotten really chummy with his wife, Rachel."

"We play mah jongg together and have clicked as friends."

"Seems like you're inseparable to me."

"I enjoy her company. Sorry, but I won't play on my relationships for something that could easily be a figment of your imagination." Morgan started to clear the table, looked at Jesse's face and stopped. "Look, the worst thing Uncle Daniel can say is no, and no is just another word like apple, or plum, or pomegranate."

"Sounds like you've got fruit on the brain. Are we having fruit for dessert?" He picked up the salad bowl and followed Morgan into the kitchen. "But you're right. Ignore paranoid little me."

"Just because you're paranoid doesn't mean they're not out to get you. And I'm not saying no because I don't want to help you. We're going over there Wednesday night for dinner. When you guys go out back for cigars, steer the conversation around to asking him." She put the dirty dishes in the sink. "And yes, we are having fruit for dessert. Peach cobbler."

"Add vanilla ice cream and I'll love you forever."

"Promises, promises."

CHAPTER 5

A full moon hovered in the southwestern night sky. Howie faced east, lying on his back, zipped into an old L.L.Bean sleeping bag, staring up at a mass of twinkling stars.

The heat of the day had not dissipated all that much. Tomorrow would be day ten of an Indian Summer heat wave gripping most of the East Coast.

Howie shivered.

The air mattress under the sleeping bag added comfort but did nothing more. Cold sweats. He'd promised his mom he'd quit. So he'd gone cold turkey, and hadn't used the entire time she was away in New Jersey. On nights he couldn't sleep he came out here, thinking the night air would help him.

Coca...cocaine. Hmmm. Nothing quite compared to the out-of-body, floating feeling. Not even sex. Howie closed his eyes and lost himself for a few moments in the euphoric memory of his last high. He licked his lips.

He was floating in a golden glow of sunlight, the cloudless sky a brilliant blue, vapor trails crisscrossing, weaving intricate patterns across the heavens. Amorphous shapes swirled before his eyes, creatures coming to life in his drug-induced haze. He raised his arms, fluttered his wings, felt himself flying. Moving, ever upward, toward the golden globe, bathing in its warmth.

Boom.

Startled awake, Howie jerked up. His heart was racing, his head spinning, his mouth dryer than a desert breeze. And he was back in his room, in his bed, with no memory of coming inside. Was his mind playing tricks on him? Had he even been outside? Was it all a dream?

He rubbed his face, swung his legs around, and wobbled to his feet, gripping the soaked sheets when he reached out to stop himself from falling. Feeling dizzy, craving sweets, he ripped open the package of Reese's Peanut Butter Cups sitting on his nightstand. The smooth peanut butter stuck to the roof of his mouth and the chocolatey sweetness tasted so good. He slid along the wall to the hall bathroom, splashed cold water on his face, and then took a piss. When he caught his reflection in the mirror he started to shake.

His life had been reduced to rubble and he had no one to blame but himself. When he did lash out—at his mother, his MIA father, his boss, his lousy jobs—the aftermath of his tirade left him empty and more despondent.

"Shit." He leaned on the vanity. "I'm such a screwup."

He took a small measure of comfort in the fact that his mother didn't know how far he'd fallen. She thought of him as her messed-up son, and, like any Jewish mother worth her salt, she blamed herself. Catholic guilt was good, but Jewish guilt was beyond good. It took on a life of its own, and, like acid reflux, it repeated and repeated.

A soft knock at the door.

"Howie, are you okay?"

He saw the doorknob jiggle.

Thank God I locked the door.

"Yeah, Mom. Be right out."

He flushed the toilet and opened the door. Sara was barefoot and wrapped in her old, ratty blue chenille robe. She went up on her toes and gave him a kiss.

"Everything okay?" She gently placed her hand on his chest.

"Sorry if I woke you."

"You didn't. I don't sleep as soundly as I used to. The trip to Jersey, being with Beth and Ellyn over the weekend, has me wired and missing them all the more."

Suddenly Sara's chest started to heave and she found herself struggling to breathe, each breath more difficult than the one before.

"Mom?"

She dropped to her knees gasping. Howie caught her before she hit the floor.

"I can't breathe." She could feel her tongue and lips swelling. "EpiPen. Night table. 911."

He gently laid her down, ran to her room, grabbed the EpiPen, ran back to her.

"I…I don't…Mom—" His hands were shaking. "I don't know how to do this."

"Blue to the sky. Orange to the thigh." Sara took the EpiPen from him, pulled off the safety cap, held the orange tip to her thigh and pushed the plunger. She massaged the injection spot while Howie ran to his room and grabbed his phone. He was back in a flash.

"911. What's your emergency?"

"My mom. She can't breathe. Send an ambulance."

"Your address?"

Howie pulled the phone away from his ear and put it on speaker. "The address…Mom…what's the address?"

"200…Willow…Lane."

"The ambulance is on the way. I'll stay on the line with you."

Howie executed a slow 360 turn to satisfy himself that he wasn't being observed. His mom. The ambulance. The hospital. It had been a horrible night, and the last thing he needed now was to be the object of anyone's attention. But it was after midnight, and the streets of Colonial Williamsburg seemed dark and deserted.

The handoff would only take a second, but caution was paramount. His buyers depended on it, and so did he. God, after almost killing his mother, he needed a hit. Bad. But business before pleasure. It hadn't taken long to find an eager buyer in this college town.

Satisfied no one was watching, he reached up, pulled off his Yankees baseball cap, and scratched his head, sending the all-clear signal across the street to whichever buyer was lurking in the shadows. Then he stepped back into the doorway alcove of the old building and waited.

It didn't take long.

He made the harried-looking guy crossing Duke of Gloucester street as his buyer. Wearing jeans, a T-shirt, and a dark, zip-up sweatshirt with the hood pulled up over his head, and clutching a backpack in his arms, the overweight guy looked like a heart attack waiting to happen.

A pang of guilt caused Howie's face to flush, but he shook it off faster than a dog shaking off bathwater. *No time for that now. What's done is done.* His mother's favorite saying, that guilt was a wasted emotion, popped in his mind. Shit, if she could see him now. What would she say about his latest scheme. Was she even still alive? Hell, she looked almost dead when the paramedics pushed her into the hospital a few hours ago.

"We good?" the man asked, approaching Howie, but not holding eye contact.

"You got the money, we're better than good."

The guy had that wild-eyed, crazy look of someone strung out on the latest drug-du-jour, wanting only to secure his next fix. He shifted the backpack to his left arm and rummaged into his right pants pocket. He pulled out a folded Benjamin and palmed it.

Howie quickly raised both of his hands to grasp the hundred dollar bill in a two-handed shake, replacing it with a tiny plastic bag containing three yellow pills.

"Nice not knowing you," said Howie, as he stepped back away from his customer and disappeared into the darkness down Botetourt Street.

"What happened?" mumbled Sara when she opened her eyes.

"You had an allergic reaction to something," said Dr. McKenna. "You're in the hospital."

Sara reached up to touch her face. "It's all a blur. How long have I been here?"

"Only overnight. It's early Wednesday. I gave you a sedative so you'd rest."

"I remember you. You're the ER doctor who tried to save the homeless man a few months back."

"You have a good memory. Have some water." She handed Sara a cup of water. "Do you remember what caused the reaction? What you ate?"

"Nothing out of the ordinary." Sara squirmed in the bed.

"What do you remember?"

Sara thought about it for a moment. "I was checking on my son. He's been staying with me for a few days. I heard noise in the hall bathroom and I wanted to make sure he was okay." Sara pushed herself up on the bed.

"Let me adjust this." Dr. McKenna took the button and raised the top of the bed. "That better?"

"Yes. Thanks." Sara took another sip of water. "I kissed him. On the lips." Sara looked at the doctor. "Peanuts. I tasted peanuts, and I'm very allergic. He must have eaten something with peanuts and the residue was on his lips, which caused the reaction."

"That'll do it. Doesn't your son know you're allergic to peanut products?"

"We haven't been around each other a lot, and my allergy has gotten worse these past few years. He only got here at the end of last week, and then I was gone for a few days."

"Okay. The paramedics brought the EpiPen you used with them. Did you know it was expired?"

"Yes, but my pharmacy was out of stock and I couldn't find a replacement."

"Smart you kept the old one. Supply has been a problem for over a year now. Something with the injector mechanism. I hope they get it fixed soon, because a lot of people are struggling to get fresh epinephrine." She went to the window. "Let me close these at bit."

"No. Please. Leave them open. I like the morning sun."

"You need to rest, but you do have one visitor who refuses to leave. She's been here all night."

"It's Rachel. Please let her come in."

"I'm in," said Rachel, rushing to the bed and giving Sara a hug. "How are you?"

"She needs to rest," said Dr. McKenna. "Short visit, please."

"I'll take care of her, Doc. Promise."

Rachel's moist eyes studied Sara. "You had me so worried. When Howie called and told me you were on your way to the ER, I rushed right over."

"I...I...It wasn't his fault. He doesn't know how bad my peanut allergy has gotten."

"It doesn't matter. The only thing that matters is that you're okay."

"I'm fine." Sara gripped Rachel's hand. She looked toward the window and then turned back to Rachel. "Rachel, do me a favor?"

"Anything."

"Howie… He must feel awful and we both know that's not good for him. Is he here?"

"No." Rachel bit her lip. "I haven't seen him since last night. He left right after I got here."

"You have to find him. I'm worried about what he'll do."

"Let me call Daniel. He'll find him. And when they release you later, you're coming home with me. No excuses."

CHAPTER 6

Standing alone, clutching the bridge's railing and staring into the darkness, Howie wasn't sure how he wound up here.

After he scored some money, he treated himself to a small hit because he needed to calm down. Then aimless driving led him here.

He remembered laughing when he pulled into the deserted parking lot. If his high-and-mighty-American-history-professor-piece-of-shit-dad could see him now. No matter. He'd hear about how his son died jumping off the bridge at Chickahominy Park and into the Chickahominy River.

Route 5 was mostly deserted this early in the morning, but he hid when a lone police cruiser drove by awhile ago. *Jump* whispered the voice inside his head. Howie rocked back and forth, then pulled himself closer to the waist-high metal rail and stared into the murky river below.

He jumped when a soft hand covered his and he turned to see a vaguely familiar face.

"Do you like who you are?"

"Stupid question. If I did, would I be getting ready to jump off this bridge?"

"Take a moment," said the man standing beside him. "The bridge and the river below aren't going anywhere. Are there times when you do like who you are?"

"There were. A long time ago. But not lately." Howie's eyes were wild when he turned to look at the man. "You don't know what I've done." Tears streamed down his face. "I killed her. Dropped her at the hospital, ran away, and didn't look back. And I just blew away the latest rehab program I claimed to have committed to."

"Your mom's fine. She's resting and Rachel's with her."

Howie pressed his fingers into his eye sockets. "How'd you know where to find me?"

"Got a call from a police friend who knew I was looking for you." Howie's glassy eyes told Daniel all he needed to know about his condition. "You didn't answer my question."

Howie looked Daniel up and down. "What's your point?"

"I think it's important for people to like who they are becoming in the everydayness of their lives. Keeps your head screwed on straight."

"My head hasn't been screwed on straight for years." Howie stared into the river below. "I'm becoming nothing. I've always been nothing." Howie chuckled. "My father, now he's something."

"He's been out of your life for years. And as for your mother…you saved her life last night."

"Shit, man. I didn't even know her address to tell 911." More tears.

"That's what brought this on, isn't it? You think you failed her, so you decided to take a little trip to Neverland?"

"Does it matter?"

"To her it does. She's frantic with worry about you. When you weren't at the hospital when she woke up, she asked Rachel to find you. Rachel called me."

"Lucky you. You found me."

"You need food. Let's go." Daniel wrapped his arm around Howie's shoulder, forcefully pulled him back from the railing, and led him toward the parking lot. "Get in. I'll drive and get your car picked up later."

They chose a booth at the back of the IHOP and each ordered the killer breakfast plate: two eggs, two meats, two pancakes, two breads, and all the coffee you could drink. Another voice drew Howie's attention away from Daniel. A handsome, bald, physically fit man with his left arm in a sling walked up to the booth and slid in next to Howie, trapping him against the wall.

"Who the hell are you?"

"I'm Moss. How are you doing?"

"What's it to you?" Howie squirmed.

"Ease up, Howie," said Daniel. "He's here to help."

Howie lowered his head into his hands, rubbed his face, let out a throaty groan, and then looked at Moss. "Who are you again?"

"Moss. A friend. Your friend, if you'll let me."

"I don't have friends, and I don't know you."

The waitress brought three coffees. Daniel picked up one of the mugs, handed it to the waitress and said, "I'll take this to go." Then, turning back to Moss and Howie, "Call if you need me."

Moss moved into Daniel's seat opposite Howie and added cream and sugar to his coffee.

"Want to know what I see?"

Howie shrugged.

"I see dilated pupils for starters, and if I push up your sleeves, I bet I'll find track marks. Maybe a few needle marks between your toes, and not a nose hair to be found inside that beak plastered between your eyes."

Howie wiped his nose, more conscious of its size than he'd been in a long time.

"You don't know anything about me."

"I know someone who loves you is freaking terrified that you're out of control."

Howie looked away, unsure what the guy would think or do if he saw tears welling up.

"Nothing to say? I'd say you're the strong, silent type, but we both know that ain't true."

"What do you want?"

"To help you get that monkey off your back."

Howie's phone buzzed. He reached for it, but Moss clamped his hand over it before Howie got to it.

"We're not done talking yet. And I don't like being interrupted."

"Whatever."

"Wrong answer."

Their eyes met, but Howie couldn't hold eye contact. He drummed his fingers on the tabletop.

"How'd you get started? With the drugs, I mean."

"High school. Chubby kid who couldn't catch a ball and tripped over his own feet. Got picked on a lot. Got me wired, couldn't sleep. Cut school. Hung out at the bowling alley. Met a guy who offered me something. Said it would help me relax. That night, I slept like a baby. When I ran into the guy again, I asked and he delivered."

"Just like that?"

"Just like that. Can I go now?" asked Howie, his tone snarky.

"What's your rush? Food's here," said Moss.

The waitress filled the table with enough food to feed an army.

"Eat," said Moss. "Then we'll talk some more. And you'll be so glad you did."

"Why's that?" Howie settled back in his seat and picked up his coffee, his hands shaking.

"Because I'm going to save your ass."

"What makes you think my ass needs saving?"

"I've seen this scenario play out before."

"Haven't we all," said Howie.

Moss could see sweat beads clustered along Howie's hairline, and saw a few trickle down the side of Howie's face before he swiped them away with his shirt sleeve.

"Your dick's caught in a wringer because you can't stay away from the stuff. There are two ways you can go. Release or squeeze. What's your choice?"

"What if I don't feel like choosing?"

"You don't feel? Feeling? Really? Feeling only goes so far and is a poor substitute for doing something to fix what's wrong."

"Nothing can fix what's wrong with me."

"Said like the schmuck you are. But you don't have to stay a schmuck. Give me action every time."

Howie took a deep breath. "I try. I really try to kick it, but it never lasts."

"Because you don't want it to. And trust me, that never ends well. Eat." Moss pointed with his fork at the plate in front of Howie, then scooped some scrambled eggs into his mouth, chewed, swallowed, and continued. "This time won't be any different unless I can reach you, convince you that doing a header off that bridge where Daniel found you isn't the answer."

"And how do you plan to do that?" Howie wolfed down the eggs on his plate like he hadn't eaten in days.

"I'm working on it." Moss buttered a piece of toast. "There are people out there who care about you, who can help you."

"Been there. Done that. Rehab doesn't work."

"It does when you want it to. And help can take many forms. I spent a lot of time not liking what I was doing and who I was being. Worked for a man who wasn't any good. He did ugly stuff and I didn't do anything to stop him."

"Why not? You look like you could take down anyone. You know, kill someone with your thumb."

"Thanks. But there were extenuating circumstances. I was trapped, kind of like you."

"Sounds mysterious. Care to elaborate?"

"In the beginning I wasn't undercover. I went to the DEA when I couldn't look at myself in the mirror anymore."

"Would make shaving treacherous," said Howie, finishing his eggs.

"The DEA. That was my version of rehab." Moss turned his attention to the sausage and bacon. "I solved my problem."

"My problem's beyond solving. I don't care anymore."

"But your mom cares. She's a good woman and you owe her more than this."

"I've been nothing but a pain in her ass for years."

Moss put down his fork, wiped his mouth, stood and ran his hand over his bald head. "When you're ready to admit you need help, call me." He tucked a card into Howie's T-shirt pocket.

Howie pulled the card out, surprised to find only a phone number printed on it. None of the usual name, rank, company information. Just a phone number, printed in black. The reverse side was blank. When he looked up again, he was alone. Moss was gone.

Daniel walked into the kitchen and wrapped his arms around Sara in a bear hug.

"Heard you had a scary night."

"That…is an understatement."

"I'm glad you're okay." He wrapped Sara in his arms again. "Anything you need?"

"No. I'm fine. Howie must have been eating peanut butter when I kissed him."

"Doesn't he know how allergic you are?"

She shook her head. "I'm not blaming him. Did you find him?"

"Yes." Daniel looked at her. All he heard was another excuse freeing her son from responsibility. But now was not the time to confront her. "He's in good hands." He grabbed a handful of raisins out of the fridge. "Why don't you stay here for a night or two? Just so we can make sure you're okay."

"I'm fine. Rachel's already asked me to stay, but I want to recover in my own home. It's got to be my safe space, my haven. And now Howie knows, so I'm sure he'll be more careful."

"How long is he staying?" asked Daniel, throwing a raisin in the air and catching it in his mouth.

"He hasn't said. And I want him to feel welcome, so I'm not going to pressure him with tons of questions. But I did lay down some ground rules, especially about the drugs."

"Good for you. Now you have to stick to them," said Rachel as she refilled everyone's coffee mugs and put a plate of piping hot cinnamon rolls on the table.

Sara smiled. "The hard part."

"What did the doctor say?" asked Daniel, pulling apart a roll and taking a bite.

"That I was lucky someone was there to call 911."

But if the dumb schmuck hadn't been eating peanut butter, the emergency wouldn't have happened. Daniel had only met Howie once before early this morning, but Rachel's stories about how he used and abused Sara had soured him on the guy. And when they met, Howie wouldn't look Daniel in the eye, which further colored his impression. In Daniel's mind, the guy was, and would always be, a loser.

"Moss just texted. He and Howie have paused their come-to-Jesus talk. He's on his way over to help me with the dock while Howie thinks things over. Do you want me to drive you home before I get all hot and sweaty?" asked Daniel.

"Nope. You're stuck with me for the day. The doctor told me to rest. Rachel and I going to play some Siamese mah jongg on the deck, and I'm staying for dinner so I can visit with Morgan and Jesse and hear all about his latest adventures reporting on the world's evils. Then you can drive me home."

Sara watched through the kitchen window as the two men laid out the dock at the river's edge.

"Tell me about Moss." Sara smoothed mustard on rye bread and piled on turkey.

"We met him a few months ago. I think he's DEA."

"What's with the on-again-off-again sling?"

"He's been working undercover on a fishing boat on the Eastern Shore and there was some trouble."

"Trouble looks like his middle name."

"He's recovering from a gunshot wound."

"Oh, my God. Is he okay?"

"He said it's just a flesh wound."

"Sling or no sling, he is one fine-looking hunk of a man." Sara felt a twitch between her legs and smiled. "Wouldn't mind causing some trouble with him. Is he staying for dinner tonight?"

"Yes, he's invited to dinner, but Sara, he's a tad young for you."

"What young? I'm still eager and he looks like he can go the distance. Don't expect he needs the little blue pill."

"You little cougar, you. You're incorrigible."

"Need a stress reliever, and he looks like just the ticket." She ran her tongue over her lips and pulled two beers out of the fridge. "Think I'll bring the guys a couple of beers."

"Tell them I've got turkey, ham, and cheese sandwiches ready whenever they are."

"I'll bet Moss is ready all the time." Sara gave Rachel a sly grin and headed out. Rachel watched her walk down the hill, her hips swaying.

CHAPTER 7

Soraya Rousseau sat in the reception area of World Health Organization Director General Ahara Obi's office. As head of the WHO, Obi was a formidable player in ensuring the one hundred and ninety-two member nations of the UN cooperated on global health initiatives.

Arranging this meeting had taken more effort than Soraya believed Obi was worth. But that was the price of doing business these days. And her annoyance was growing exponentially the longer she waited. The minutes were ticking by. Thirty so far. That would soon end.

The door to the Director General's inner sanctum opened and a tall woman in an expensively tailored navy blue suit, and with enviable thick, black, curly hair, approached.

"Ms. Rousseau. I'm Renata Johnson, Director General Obi's Chief of Staff and legal counsel. So nice to finally meet you. I am so sorry for the delay. The Director has been on the phone with the Secretary General of the UN, and as I'm sure you can understand, you can't rush these conversations. As you know, the World Health Organization does very important work, so when the Secretary General calls, it is imperative that he not be kept waiting."

"Of course. I totally understand."

"Please follow me." She turned and led the way, then elegantly pirouetted back to face Soraya, saying, "I'm afraid your meeting today will have to be short and to the point. The Director General's schedule has gotten backed up a bit. I do hope you can be concise so your meeting produces the outcomes you want."

"I am nothing if not concise in all my business dealings."

Ms. Johnson opened the mahogany door and ushered Soraya into the Director General's office with its spectacular view of the city. When Pierre Charles L'Enfant designed Washington, DC, his intent was to force anyone who might seek to do the United States harm to think twice. This building, with its fancy rotunda entrance, broadcast that message loud and clear, though Soraya could think of a thousand better uses for the space. A tall, slender, well-dressed, lawyerly-looking woman, her gray hair tightly trapped in a bun at the nape of her neck, hung up the phone and rose from behind her desk as Soraya approached.

"Ms. Rousseau, how nice to meet you."

"You too, Director."

"You don't mind if my assistant Renata joins us, do you?" said Obi as Renata headed for a seat.

"To be truthful, I do mind." As Soraya spoke, she lightly touched Renata's elbow and gently escorted her toward the door. "My business today is rather confidential, if you must know. I prefer a private meeting—which is what you agreed to when we first spoke. I'm sure you can fill Ms. Johnson in on any details you believe to be pertinent after I leave."

Director Obi swallowed hard, and her eyes darted left and then right as she probably wondered what topic would necessitate her guest's insistence on absolute privacy.

"As you wish. That will be all, Renata. Please hold my calls. Oh, and give me a five-minute heads-up so I'm not late for my meeting with Senator Whitley."

Renata's cold stare and icy smile were directed at Soraya. To her boss she said, "Of course, ma'am." The two women remained standing and silent as an indignant Renata Johnson strode out of the room.

"That was a rather unfortunate way to begin our relationship, Ms. Rousseau. Renata sits in on all of my meetings to take notes."

"Then let this be the start of a new tradition. And since she alerted me to the tightness of your schedule today, I'll get right to the point."

Soraya stood in front of the Director's oversized mahogany desk, removed an envelope from her Prada attaché case, and handed it to Obi.

"What's this?"

"Information."

The Director opened the envelope and unfolded the stiff white linen stationary contained within. Putting on her reading glasses, she read the three short paragraphs of information. The sheet dropped from her hand.

"You can't be serious."

"Totally. Do I have your full attention now?"

Her "yes" was barely audible.

"Good. I thought we might see eye to eye on this topic. And aren't you glad I insisted on a private meeting? You may share whatever you want to share with Ms. Johnson. I don't expect it will be much...or the truth. Feel free to make up whatever lie best serves you."

Director Obi remained dumbstruck. "But how?"

"You don't need to know how, only that we have pictures. Glorious, full color, career-ending pictures. Information like this...were it to find its way into the wrong hands..."

"I was young." Obi stiffened. "Just...just following orders. You don't know what it was like back then."

"The photos tell a different story. Looks like you are the one giving the orders." Soraya could see the woman tense. "Do I make myself clear?"

"Yes. What is it you want?"

"Your full cooperation regarding certain medical cargo shipments about to enter your country that are not to be stopped or waylaid from their final destinations. We don't want any complications with Congolese customs once the shipment arrives in Kinshasa—or any other country's customs, for that matter."

"Is that all?"

"Yes. Easy, isn't it? Similar shipments will be arriving at other entry points in Mumbai, Ottawa, and Mexico City. None are to be stopped, searched, or scrutinized in any way whatsoever."

"But there are protocols."

"Protocols can be circumvented. And we're confident that you have it within your power to make this happen." Soraya picked up a small glass globe of the world. "A paperweight? From Tiffany, if I'm not mistaken. I have one just like it on my desk."

"Your point?"

"You have expensive taste, and live well, unlike many of your countrymen who barely have indoor plumbing and clean water. It would be a shame to lose all of this over…over…over such a trivial matter and the small request I am making today."

Soraya's friendly smile belied the seriousness of Director Obi's situation. The media was having a field day reporting numerous failures of critical medications worldwide over the past few years because of contamination. Uncontrollable outbreaks of highly contagious coronavirus-type diseases like SARS and H1N1, deadly hemorrhagic fevers like Ebola, and other emergencies threatened to further reduce voluntary contributions from philanthropists. America's president was threatening to pull funding from the WHO, and the growing tariff war with China were proof that his threats were not to be ignored. The United States was the WHO's single largest contributor, funds the Director couldn't afford to put in jeopardy.

"And if I don't cooperate?"

"Use your imagination." Soraya's bright red fingertips gently touched the stiff white letter lying on Obi's desk. "Agencies of the UN have had more than their share of scandalous exploitation cases recently. Would you like to see your name associated with the next one?"

Obi cleared her throat and slumped into her chair. "There are dedicated men and women, medical professionals, who are clamoring to help the poorest among us, who are constantly ravaged by diseases too horrible to imagine. This might be a bridge too far, even for me."

"And yet, Director, we both know you are a very powerful person at the UN, leading a very powerful agency. You've risen very high, especially for a woman from an African country that thinks of women as chattel. I know you have aspirations beyond the World Health Organization. The first female Secretary General, perhaps? That would be a major coup for a woman, and a black woman at that. I'm confident you can find a way to circumvent customs as we have requested. You've been handsomely paid for years, and now it's time to earn your money."

Soraya's piercing green eyes briefly left the Director's face. She looked down at the letter sitting on the desk, then looked back up at Obi. "For your sake. It would be a shame to see such an esteemed reputation as yours tarnished by anything as untoward as this."

The two women stared at each other. In a different venue the climate would have been ripe for a brutal catfight. Soraya could see the perspiration forming on Obi's brow. She could almost feel the sweat rolling down the back of the woman's neck.

"And so unnecessary. Let's be ladies about this." Soraya picked up the letter and replaced it in the envelope. "Know that we're watching. I'll be calling you from time to time to let you know what additional actions you need to take and where. It really will be quite painless for you, and quite profitable in the long term."

A heavy silence hung in the room like a dense fog.

Comfortable that she had made the required impression, Soraya smiled. "Thank you for your time, Director Obi. We'll be watching your progress on this endeavor. And it goes without saying that we'll be in touch as the need arises."

Soraya quietly left a stunned Director Obi sitting behind her big, important desk. She walked down the hall, stopped at the door with a sign that showed it to be the office of Ms. Johnson.

Opening the door after the courtesy of a brief double knock, Soraya said, "She's all yours."

Renata Johnson donned her suit jacket, walked down the hall to Director Obi's office, and knocked softly.

"Come."

"Is everything okay?"

"You took your sweet time getting down here. I figured you'd be camped outside my door, maybe with a glass to the wall to see if you could hear what was said."

"Director Obi, I...I assure you I would never betray your trust in me by doing such a thing."

"Of course you wouldn't."

The director locked eyes with Renata. Her mind reeled with a number of ways to hurt this poor excuse for a human being, but now was not the time. She'd found the listening devices months ago when her suspicions were aroused because private conversations were becoming public too frequently. The technician who swept her office was able to determine the receiver was in Renata's office. Obi'd left the equipment in place but took precautions.

The topic of her visit with Ms. Rousseau had surprised her. Unfortunately, the conversation and subsequent threat, coupled with Renata's removal from the meeting, were sure to intensify her curiosity. How to deal with her was the least of Obi's problems. Should photos of her past surface, Obi knew her career would be over and possible war crimes charges could be filed.

"It was much ado about nothing."

"I'm...I'm glad to hear that." Renata smoothed the front of her skirt and turned to go. "Is there anything I can do for you?"

"Not right now. But please cancel my appointments for the rest of the day. I'll be leaving shortly."

"Do you want me to come with you?"

"That won't be necessary."

"Are you sure? You seem upset. Whatever did that woman say to you?"

"Renata, I know you see yourself assuming the directorship of the WHO should I be successful in acquiring the votes necessary from the required nine security council members to be promoted to Secretary General by the General Assembly. And I do appreciate your efforts on my behalf, especially those that derail plots against my leadership. The UN is a hotbed of political intrigue, fiefdoms, and small-minded men from nowhere countries vying for prominence. But let's not rush things. All in good time."

CHAPTER 8

"I hear you had an interesting trip," said Daniel when he and Jesse took their wine and walked out to the deck after dinner. Moss had volunteered to drive Sara home, and Morgan was helping Rachel with kitchen duty.

"It was fun."

"Africa? Fun? Nothing like walking on the wild side. What happened to sand and sun vacations?"

"Wasn't a vacation. More of a research trip. Accepted a freelance gig. Started out about the incessant civil wars and strife in so many countries and what they're doing to the local populations."

"Started about that? Pray tell, what did it end with?"

"I'm not sure yet. I'll do the war story for the magazine since that's what they're paying me to write, but Morgan and I are working on something else that I think is much more explosive."

"I can see that mischievous twinkle in your eye from here."

"You know me too well."

"I know how you like to push the envelope and make waves, but I also see sadness. Want to talk about it?"

"I met this great kid who died of an infection and no one

seemed to give a shit. A boy is dead. Thousands of innocent boys and girls...children are dead...or maimed...and the killing is endless. It has to stop."

"Crusader Jesse rides to the rescue."

"It got more interesting when I hit the Congo. You name the disease and it's there. I can understand dying from Ebola, but I couldn't understand why so many people were dying from malaria when there are very effective drugs available. I really ruffled a few feathers when I started asking 'why' questions of the WHO representatives and Congolese leaders at a press conference."

"That could prove dangerous. Most countries are not as benevolent with the press as we are. And the Congo has been mired in an internal bloodbath for years. The Congolese don't take well to outside interference, especially from white American journalists. You could disappear or get eaten by a lion."

"It's what I do," said Jesse. "What I was born to do." He smiled and sipped his wine. "I am the great disruptor. I poke my nose where it doesn't belong, ask questions that disrupt the status quo, and make people very uncomfortable, especially people who have something to hide."

"What do you think they're hiding? What were you asking questions about?"

"Genocide."

"Excuse me?"

"Collateral damage is probably a nicer term, more politically correct. I'm investigating the ramifications of years of civil war on the health and well-being of third world populations. In addition to the rapes and outright killings by rogue men roaming the countryside, there are people dying by the thousands in the third world from diseases that have cures. Malaria, cholera, dengue, Ebola. I could go on, but I think you get the picture."

"Interesting." Daniel took a metal scrub brush and started to scrape the grill grates. "I think you may have been out of the country, but a few weeks ago Border Patrol caught some Congolese wading across the Rio Grande to seek asylum. Not sure how they got the money to travel from Africa to Mexico, but Border Patrol agents stopped them. Imagine the problem if someone carrying a communicable disease like Ebola was to get in illegally."

"At least here we have the drugs to treat them."

"But with the craziness at the southwestern border, if they got into the country without showing symptoms and disappeared, or were sent somewhere, we could have a public health nightmare on our hands before we even knew what hit us. What made you start investigating this?"

"My crass side says money. Killing two birds with one stone. I was already there, and I think this story might be a winner that a news organization will be happy to pay big bucks for."

"Or someone could pay big bucks to have it silenced."

Jesse scowled at Daniel. "Last year, the thing with Eli and the homeless dying when someone was stealing their kidneys? The black market organ-trafficking episode opened my eyes to the value people from different parts of the world place on human life. Don't get me wrong. I don't have a naive bone in my body, and I know poverty's a worldwide problem, but uncovering a black market organ ring right here in Williamsburg, stealing kidneys from the homeless, sickened me."

"We were lucky we got to that clinic in time."

"Darby was the really lucky one. She could have died, and her little girl would have been an orphan."

"Jesse, are you getting sentimental on me?"

"No. When Morgan and I were writing that story, our research took us outside Williamsburg. Learning that there's an entire city in India with people willing to sell a kidney for pennies to feed their families astonished me. One article led to another, and I was hooked. Had to go see it for myself. Found an assignment that would pay my way. Hence the trip."

"What did you learn?"

"That there are thieving bastards, most notably politicians, and other power-hungry people of all sizes, colors, and shapes everywhere."

"Now that sounds more like the Jesse I know and have come to love."

"Morgan and I are just beginning to sift through my notes and the tapes of interviews from this trip. Not sure where it will lead us, but we both agreed to write the story that emerges from the recordings."

"If there's anything I can do to help…"

Jesse gazed out into space for a few moments. "Since you offered, there is one thing. I think I picked up a tail. Not sure why, but the same car seems to be following me pretty much everywhere I go."

"How do you know it's the same one?"

"When I told Morgan about it, she said I was imagining things. And I know black SUVs are very common, but there's something about this one that gets the hairs on the back of my neck standing at full attention."

"Ah, instincts. Guess reporters are like cops and get a gut kick when something is off." Daniel finished cleaning the grill and closed the lid. "Where did this happen last?"

"Richmond Road. By the McDonalds. I turned off onto Monticello, then went into the parking lot by Rita's Ice and drove out by the Goodwill. Thought I lost him because I didn't see him in the rearview mirror. I made a left and then another right back onto Richmond Road. And the SUV popped up in my rearview mirror by the time I got to Zable Stadium."

"You're beginning to sound like a native. Zable Stadium?"

"The stadium on Richmond Road just before the Historic District."

"I don't go driving around over there. Too many college kids with their noses glued to their phones and not watching where they're going."

"I got the plate number," said Jesse, digging into his pocket and pulling out a piece of paper. "Diplomatic plates. SAA 0456. Can you run it for me?"

"I'll see what I can do." Daniel wiggled his fingers and Jesse handed him the paper.

"It's late. Come to bed."

"A few more minutes." Morgan looked away from her laptop when Jesse started tickling her behind her ear. "What are you doing?"

"Causing trouble."

She closed the laptop, placed it on the coffee table, and reached up and pulled Jesse to her, locking her lips onto his. "Hmm. I like trouble. Trouble tastes good."

He slid over the back edge of the sofa, landing on her lap. "You want to mess around?"

"Sure. I'm game." Holding his face between her hands, she planted soft, butterfly kisses along his cheek and nibbled at his lips.

Jesse was different from most of the men who crossed her path. He was easygoing, unpretentious, and sure of himself without being cocky. He had a great laugh and a smile that lit up his entire face.

Any story they worked on together came in fits and starts as their pile of research grew. What she loved most about their collaborations was that he listened to her ideas and asked her opinion. Most guys she'd done projects with before took the lead, gave her the grunt work, and hogged the limelight when it was time to collect the accolades.

Jesse also didn't look like the type women lusted after in romance novels, not a sexy hunk with bedroom eyes. He was your reliable lab partner, the guy next door who had every tool, the fun guy at parties. Morgan felt safe with him.

But every once in a while, when they'd been working extra hard in close quarters, he'd give her a look and something would kick inside her. Even during their first date over coffee at Barnes & Noble in Merchants Square something had charged the air between them. Attraction?

He sat up and started kissing her furiously. "I'll give you trouble." His lips found hers again while his hands started roaming her body.

"Not fair." She squirmed and giggled with delight.

"Whoever promised you fair?"

"You did when you moved down here." She pushed him off her lap and reached for her computer.

"You've been hooked up to your computer since we got back from Daniel and Rachel's. What are you working on?" Jesse twisted around so he could read what was on the screen.

"Drugs."

"Planning on doing a little medicated flying?"

"No. Getting high isn't my thing. I'm high on life."

He reached for her and planted another warm kiss on her neck.

"Stop, please. Get serious."

"Why? This is much more fun."

"Granted." She put the laptop down and wrapped her arms around his neck. "One good kiss and then it's back to work."

"If we must, but I prefer to mess around. I missed you."

"Baltimore was only overnight."

"But before that I was gone for two months. We've got some catching up to do."

The kiss was a good one, tongues poking and prodding, his hands moving under her shirt, fingers finding her nipples.

"Okay. Enough."

"If you insist." He changed position to sit next to her and folded his hands in his lap. "Now what's got you hooked?"

"Drugs. I told you."

"Care to be more specific?"

"You started it with the two vials you brought back from the Congo. Got me curious."

"Curious is dangerous."

"This article," she said, pointing to her computer screen, "is reporting on a rash of deaths from malaria in sub-Saharan Africa."

"Marcel didn't die from malaria. It was an infection."

"I know. But there may be correlations. The authorities suspect the malaria drugs weren't the real thing."

"Which authorities?"

"The World Health Organization. And those guys should know since they monitor health incidents worldwide."

"WHO? The UN? Talk about an organization whose demise is long overdue. I can think of a thousand and one better uses for that New York real estate."

"Come on. The UN is trying to make a difference in the world."

"Who are you?" Jesse gave her a cockeyed stare. "What did you do with cynical, suspicious-of-everyone-and-everything, skeptical Morgan, the woman I love?"

Morgan laughed and threw a pillow at him, but her mind was riveted on the last few words of his question. *Woman I love?*

"Won't be the first time tainted drugs killed people," said Jesse. "Remember the heparin mess?"

"No. When was that?"

"2008. I remember because it was right when my dad died. I was sure…am still sure…the hospital screwed up. And a few months later all this stuff came out about contaminated heparin."

"What did you do?"

"Couldn't do much of anything. My mom was still alive and dad was gone. I wasn't about to suggest digging him up and demanding toxicology tests."

"Did he take heparin?"

"Not specifically. Heparin is used in surgeries to prevent clotting. God, I must have read every article written about the stuff. Did you know it's made from pig intestines?"

"Never heard of it before, so obviously I didn't know that. In 2008 I had just started with *the Beacon,* so I was probably stuck in garden club hell and writing obituaries."

"My dad, the religious Jew. That's what he gets for using pork products."

"Not funny, Jesse."

"Sure it is." Jesse stood and held out his hand to her. "Come on. Let's go to bed. It's late. You can finish this in the morning."

Morgan shut the lid of her laptop and got up. "What happened with the heparin?"

"Government got involved. It was eventually traced back to a pig farm in China that had never been inspected."

"Did other people die?"

"Yep. Well over fifty. And some kids, too, who were taking heparin as part of their dialysis routine."

"Do you think it's still happening?"

"Without a doubt. I think that's what killed Marcel. Not heparin specifically, but a bad drug. And I think I'll have proof once I get the lab results from my friend."

"When did he say he'd get back to you?"

"He told me to give him a few days. But the article you're reading, combined with the vials I brought back, proves that there's something very rotten in the pharmaceutical world, beyond companies making tons of money by charging outrageous prices."

"I'm not liking this," Morgan smiled at him. "But you're right. It's time for bed." She could see Jesse's face take on a serious expression.

"Morgan, do me a favor."

"Of course."

"Vary your routine."

She gave him a questioning look, and he turned to her and drew her into his arms, then leaned back, keeping his hands on her arms.

"This whole thing with the guy at the airport and the black SUV… Until we know more, change up what you do, where you go, how you get there."

Morgan bit her tongue, resisting the temptation to smart-mouth him, claim her independence, deny him in the name of women's rights. But she stopped herself when she saw the softness in his eyes. *He cares about me.*

"I can do that."

"Thank you." He pulled her closer. "And thank you for not fighting me on this. I know how hard it'll be for you to do this favor for me."

CHAPTER 9

"How did things go after I left?" Soraya asked as soon as Renata answered her call. She slipped out of her shoes, poured a glass of champagne, and enjoyed one of the hors d'oeuvres the hotel management had left in her suite.

"You certainly got her attention. I've never seen Obi so rattled. She had me cancel the rest of her appointments and raced out of here."

"Your information was outstanding. And alluding to photos shook her to her core. Who knew the magic of the word 'photography.' Makes my heart flutter."

It would if you had a heart, thought Renata. "How much longer do you need me to spy on her?"

"Not much longer. Deliveries are proceeding here without too many obstacles. Deliveries elsewhere remain trouble free. The Ebola outbreak in the Congo has caused a few ripples, but nothing our suppliers can't handle, especially with you alerting us to upcoming inspections. Keep up the good work, sister, and all your dreams will come true."

"That's easy for you to say. You're roaming free, not cooped up in an office doing menial work for a sycophantic bitch."

"Calm yourself, sister. It will all be worth it in the end."

"What is our next step?"

"Infiltration of the American supply chain. It's been more difficult because of strict FDA rules, but rules are made to be broken. And the more rules there are, the easier it is to find rebels who resent the constraints. The more Americans clamor for cheaper drugs, the easier our work will be."

"We can't get too complacent. The FDA can be a formidable adversary."

"Pooh." Soraya had a thought. "Perhaps you'd like a change of scene? Maybe we could arrange an opportunity at the FDA?"

"Trading one huge bureaucracy for another doesn't interest me in the least. I want to be with you, like the old days. Out in the field, stoking confusion, driving men crazy."

"And so you shall, my sweet. Soon."

Soraya ended the call, slouched back against the sofa cushions, and gazed out at the White House. Their reunion had been sweet, and now might prove bittersweet, should Renata want more than Soraya was willing to offer. She got up and poured herself another glass of champagne. Sipping it slowly, she realized that there were bigger issues at stake, and Renata could prove to be a problem that would need solving.

It was after the lunch rush, so the Longhorn wasn't crowded when Howie walked in. He didn't know the man he was meeting, but when he looked around he decided it had to be the guy sitting alone in a booth at the back of the restaurant. The guy stood when Howie approached.

"Howie, my man." He held out his hand. "Thanks for meeting me. Glad you didn't have any trouble finding the place."

"My mom lives not too far away, and I picked up a six-pack at the Publix across the parking lot."

"Hope you're hungry. They do a killer ribeye here. I already ordered for us, medium rare, baked potatoes with all the fixings, and corn fritters. I told the girl to bring you a Coors and put the order in when she sees you. Hope that's okay."

"Yeah. Sure."

The waitress set his Coors down. "Your lunch will be out shortly."

"Thanks." He waved away the frosted glass.

"What do I call you?" asked Howie, taking a sip of the frosty cold beer.

"Oh. Where are my manners?" The man gave his forehead a light tap with the palm of his hand. "I'm Bob...Bob Smith."

They chatted about nothing while they ate. The server cleared their dirty plates and brought them coffee and the check, which Bob pulled toward him.

"I guess we should get down to business."

"Whatever. It's your party."

"Do you understand what to do?"

"Yeah. Don't worry. I got this covered."

"Review it for me," said Bob. "Just so I'm sure we're both on the same page."

"I go to the storage facility on Mooretown Road. Get there by ten. They're foreclosing on a few storage units for unpaid rent. And I bid on the one you want."

"I don't want it. My employer does."

"And who's he?"

"Howie, we work on a need-to-know basis. And my employer's name is something that, at this point in our relationship, you don't need to know. Think of this outing as a first date. If you do your job well, and we hope you do, we'll have more dates. Eventually, once trust has been established, I'm confident my employer will want to meet you."

Bob slid his hand across the table to Howie, a scrap of paper concealed under his palm. "That's the unit number. Take your time. Don't look overly eager. Maybe bid on one or two units before this one." He tapped the paper.

"Yeah. Sure. Fake 'em out."

Bob rolled his eyes, then spoke sternly. "Come through for us and there'll be other opportunities. You'll be rolling in it, beyond your wildest dreams.

"I got some pretty wild dreams."

"And with your share, you'll be in a position to make all of your dreams come true."

"When does the job go down?"

"Saturday." Bob put three twenties on top of the check. "Howie, listen up. This is a legitimate auction. Don't go getting ahead of yourself. Keep a low profile. When that unit comes up, do your thing. We figure you should be able to get it for under five thousand, but you're authorized to go to ten."

"Five thousand dollars? That's a lot of money. What the hell is in the unit? Gold?"

"Don't trouble yourself with minor details."

"What happens once I get the unit?"

"You take possession." Bob slid a padlock, key, and a thick white envelope across the table. "You can keep or sell whatever is in the unit, except for what we want."

"How will I know the difference? What you want and what I can sell?"

"What we want we'll take within twenty-four hours. After you complete the sale, call this number, lock the unit, and leave." He stood up, reached into his pocket, and handed Howie a black business card with a phone number printed in white ink. No name. No address. Just a number.

"We'll be watching, and I'll be in touch to get any

change." Smith pointed at the envelope and pulled out his cell phone when it beeped. "I've got to take this call. Stay here for five minutes. Get another cup of coffee or another beer. We'll talk soon." He took a step, but paused and turned back. "And Howie. Don't screw up."

Howie watched him walk out of the restaurant, but didn't see him get into any car in the parking lot, even though he was watching out the front window.

"Smith." Bob walked to a blind corner of the building to watch the comings and goings at the front door.

"How was lunch?" asked the voice on the other end of the phone line.

"Morton's steak house it isn't, but what can you expect for twenty bucks?"

"And our little friend? How's he? Think he can pull this off?"

"Yeah, Ms. Rousseau." Bob ran his hand around his chin and took a deep breath. "The boy needs a home, a family, somewhere to belong. And he wants more work from us, so I anticipate he can handle a simple buy."

"That's what we thought about the last guy."

"True. But the last guy had issues that went way deeper than Howie's mommy issues. This guy's desperate to prove to his mother than he's not a loser, that he can be somebody."

"I had mommy issues once."

"How'd you handle it?"

"She had an unfortunate accident in her bathtub. End of issue."

"Hey, girl. How was the rest of your weekend?" asked Jasmine when Debra McKenna opened the door to the lab.

"Did you two hit the hot spots of downtown Williamsburg?"

"What hot spots?"

"Got me," laughed Jasmine. "I'm married."

"Sunday was perfect. Neither of us cares much for the high life. We had a quiet day, a nice dinner, and curled up in front of the fire pit watching the sunset over the reservoir. It's nice to slow down since both of us work jobs that only go warp speed."

"Sounds romantic to me. And...fireworks? You two doing the horizontal hula yet?"

"Jasmine, that is none of your business, and I wouldn't tell you if we were."

"The smile on your face is telling me all I need to know."

"What I need to know is if you've finished testing that insulin sample I dropped off on Saturday night."

"Sorry for the delay. Olivia got hit with the flu bug so I needed to take a few sick days to stay with her." Jasmine opened a file folder and pulled out a document. "It was insulin all right, but compromised. Did you notice it was cloudy?"

"Yes." Debra turned her attention to the one-page report Jasmine handed her. "Since the guy Mrs. Lee bought it from had it in a cooler I'm guessing it wasn't stored properly."

"That *and* it was out of date. Double whammy. Of course the woman couldn't have known that from looking at the vial. I ran a check of the lot number from the label. It was part of a stolen batch of insulin from two years ago."

"No wonder poor Lette didn't get better. Can you send me the lot number so I can pass it on to Detective Knight?"

"Already done. Check your email. And I reported it to the FDA. Did they find the guy who sold it?"

"Adam thinks he talked to the guy late Saturday at the flea market and he's checking him out."

"That's good news."

"Yes. He's going back on Saturday and bringing Mrs. Lee, hoping she'll identify him."

"Won't that be dangerous for her?"

"No. She'll be with a plainclothes officer and kept at a distance. All she needs to do is finger the guy as the one who sold her the insulin. Then they can bring him in for questioning and get a warrant to search his home and truck."

CHAPTER 10

"How's Howie's visit going?" asked Rachel when she and Sara were on the back deck, playing Siamese mah jongg the next day.

"Same ol', same ol'. Nothing new there." Sara sipped her wine while Rachel mixed the tiles. "He's got a new scam he's excited about."

"What's it this time?"

"Ever watch the program *Storage Wars*?"

"Nope. Reality TV isn't my thing."

"Right. You're the book queen." Sara finished racking and arranging her tiles. "Ready?"

"Sure. You would think starting with twenty-seven tiles I'd get a joker. But no. No jokers for me."

"West," said Sara. The tile hit the table and Rachel took her turn. "Anyway, the program is about these people who bid on storage lockers that have gone into default. They only get a quick peek at what's inside each unit. Then they have to bid."

"Trash or treasures. Sounds like a waste of money."

"Not necessarily. When I've watched the program, some of the buyers find stuff they can sell for a lot of money."

"Which is, I'm assuming, what attracted Howie," said Rachel.

"Yep. Howie's the king of easy money. Always looking for a shortcut. He's going to an auction Saturday at a facility on Mooretown Road and he's sure he's going to hit it big."

"Seven bam."

"Take," said Sara. She put the tile on top of her rack and added three other seven bams to it. "Unfortunately, none of his get-rich-quick schemes ever work out, which cycles him into depression, which then feeds his drug habit."

"I'm sorry. I know how stressful this is for you."

The two continued taking turns, picking tiles, throwing tiles, working on building their hands.

"It's just that…hell, I don't know what it is. Howie has a secret life that's entirely unknown to me. He calls on rare occasions, visits when it suits him, usually when he needs money. I know he does drugs, probably deals too. And now this storage shed fiasco. What am I supposed to do? The guy needs a good job and someone in his life who's a steady influence."

"Moss could be that person."

"Moss?" Sara cleared her throat, struggling to stifle a grin. "The guy helping Daniel build the dock?"

"One and the same. The dock's almost done, and then he'll have nothing to do. He helped Daniel look for Howie the other night, so he and Howie have already met."

"Not possible," said Sara. "When he drove me home, we got to talking. One thing led to another and I asked him what he did. He said he travels a lot. Wasn't much of an answer, but Howie needs someone who'll be around for a while."

"And he will be. The doctor ordered him to be still for a few weeks. He's staying with us, so he does have time to be around for Howie."

"Maybe I should take you up on your offer to stay at your house. It might be interesting having Moss close by."

"Sara! Get your mind back on track. We're talking about Howie's problems, not your horniness."

"Give a girl a break. You've got a wonderful man. I'm lonely. One can dream."

"Back to Howie, please."

"If only Howie would cooperate." Sara picked a tile, blew out a breath and started doing her sitting down happy dance. "Double mahj jongg. Both racks. Jokerless. Ooh, big money. Pay up."

Howie bounced up and down on his heels, jumpy like he had ants in his pants. He knew there'd be people at the auction, but he hadn't expected this large a crowd. There were ten lockers up for grabs to the highest bidders.

Let the games begin, thought Howie, sizing up his fellow bidders as they walked to the first locker.

"Gather 'round folks," said Murray the auctioneer, a short, beefy guy with a well-endowed beer belly, gray hair and a full Santa-style beard. "Y'all know this is a cash transaction, so I hope you've brought plenty of dough to make your dreams come true. Never know what you're gonna find. You've got three minutes to check 'er out. Course you can't go inside, so get yourself a good viewing spot." He looked over the fifty-plus people, mostly men, who had followed him down the aisle to locker twelve. "Open 'er up."

His helper, a younger version of himself, broke the lock with bolt cutters and lifted the metal door. The crowd pressed forward. Howie cranked his head and maneuvered his way to the front of the group.

He saw some ratty old furniture, several metal filing cabinets, children's toys and bicycles.

Nope. Not this one.

The bidding was between two guys in jeans and Jimmy Buffett T-shirts. In less than two minutes the bidding ended at three hundred dollars and the crowd walked to the next unit.

Seven units later, Howie could feel the cash burning a hole in his pocket. None of the lockers looked like they contained any prizes. Most had house furnishings, old appliances, and toys. Not interested.

"Here we are, folks, unit seventy-five. It's a beauty. Just to give you some history, this one's a fairly new rental. Guy paid the first month, moved his stuff in, but hasn't paid anything since. Kinda like he fell off the face of the earth. Three months is the limit on past due. Think the owner might have died, but who knows? We'll start the bidding at one hundred dollars after your three-minute sneak peek."

Unit seventy-five. This is the one. My golden ticket. Howie's eyes popped when the door slid up.

"Now that's what I'm talking about." Pure delight sizzled from his head to his toes. He could see sporting equipment, barbells, two army-green footlockers, a set of four tires that looked to have usable tread, two tall metal cabinets, and dozens of large cartons. There was a wooden four-panel room divider screen halfway in, so it was hard to see what was behind it, but everything looked to be in good shape.

"Let's start the bidding at one hundred dollars. Who's gonna get it going?"

"One fifty," said one of the two women in the group.

"Two hundred," yelled out someone else.

"Two twenty-five," another called out.

"Three hundred," said Howie, wanting into the game.

His high bid didn't last long. One by one bidders raised the previous bid in increments of twenty-five and fifty dollars. Finally, Howie couldn't stand the tension. "One thousand dollars."

"I see we got a player," said the auctioneer. "Can I get eleven hundred?"

Murmurs rippled through the crowd, but no one countered.

"Going once…going twice…going three times… Sold." He banged his hand against the metal door frame. "Step forward young man. It's all yours. Congratulations."

The other bidders moved on and Howie found himself alone and staring at the gunmetal gray corrugated steel door, behind which were belongings he now owned. Rollers groaned as Howie strained to slide up the door. He ran his fingers through his hair, then parked his hands on his hips, his thoughts a thousand miles away. He had twenty-four hours to clean the unit out or sign rental papers and start paying for it.

Bob Smith and his invisible partners intruded on his euphoria. *What items in this unit are they after?* He pulled out his cell phone and the card with the number he was supposed to call.

The switchblade popped open in front of Howie's eyes.

"Want some help?"

"Moss. I thought I saw you in the crowd, but when I looked again you were gone." Howie remembered the card Moss had given him and suddenly realized it was formatted exactly like the card Bob Smith handed him at Longhorn. Both were totally blank except for a phone number. Moss's was white with black ink while Bob's was black with white numbers. *Gotta get me some cards just like 'em.*

Howie glanced around to make sure he wasn't being watched, then he put his cell away. The call could wait until he was alone.

"I come and go really fast." Moss smiled at him and walked into the storage shed. "Looks like you've bought yourself quite a prize."

"Hope so." Howie moved through the narrow aisle of boxes, watching Moss's every move.

"This screen alone is worth what you paid for the entire lot," said Moss. "If I'm not mistaken, it's late Qing Dynasty, the last dynasty of China. After that it became the Republic of China."

"How do you know that?"

"I travel a lot. Spent a lot of time in Asia. Back then the people were eager to display their newfound wealth, so they bought expensive hand-carved furnishings to show off. The wood's teak, and the carvings symbolize offerings of wealth for the owner." With that, Moss peeked behind the screen. "Holy shit!"

Howie came to his side.

"Now that's what I call a real prize." Moss pulled at his chin. "A 1950 Indian Chief. Do you know how much this beauty is worth?"

"No."

"Easily over twenty from a collector." Moss walked around the bike. "It's got a 74-cubic-inch flathead engine, left-hand twist grip, foot clutch, four-speed gear box, and it's bitchin' red."

"Score!" Howie held up his hand for a high five. His mouth watered. *Shit, I hope the cycle isn't what Bob's boss wants, or else it'll be gone and I'll lose all that money.*

"I may even think about making you an offer. She's a beauty."

"Guess I did good. If I can sell this screen and it's worth what you say it is, I'll recoup my money. Everything else is gravy. And I've got all these boxes to go through. Who knows what I'll find in them?"

"I've got a friend who might be interested in the bike. Let me give him a call. Be right back." Moss walked out of the shed and disappeared down the aisle.

When Moss was out of earshot, Howie pulled out his cell, punched in the number, and when Bob answered he told him the deal was done. Bob told him to leave the unit alone until tomorrow morning, at which time everything remaining would be his to do with as he pleased.

Howie disconnected and surveyed his possessions.

"Can't call me a loser now, can you, Mom?"

"Who you talking to?" asked Moss when he appeared at Howie's side.

"No one. Just shouting from the rooftops is all. I did good."

"Can't reach my friend," said Moss walking over to the wall of boxes, "but I'll keep trying. Meantime, let's check out some of these boxes." Moss flicked open the switchblade, dipped the point into the tape, and sliced one box open.

"Hold up there," said Howie, remembering Bob's orders to leave everything untouched.

"What's the problem?" Moss eyed him curiously. "Don't you want to see what's in all these boxes?"

"Yeah… Sure… But it's getting late and I promised my mom I'd meet her for lunch."

"Lunch time is long past." While he was talking Moss flipped up the box's lid.

"Come on, man. All this can wait." Howie pushed the box lid shut and tried to get the tape to stick. "I've got stuff to do now. I'm coming back tomorrow with a truck to take everything out."

"Why? Just stop at the office on your way out and pay a month's rent on the unit. It'll take you that long to sort through all this stuff."

"Whatever. Let's go." Howie walked away, hoping Moss would follow him.

His impatience surprised Moss, whose hand was back inside the box.

"What have we got here?" He pulled out a small box to read the fine print.

"Drop that." Howie nervously raced up to Moss, grabbed what was in his hand and dropped it back in the carton. "Good idea to rent the unit for a month. Think I'll lock up and go to the office and do just that. You coming? Or do you want to spend the night locked in here?"

"Right behind you." Moss stared at the contents of the open box and eyed the wall of boxes with similar markings.

When they got outside, Howie pulled down the shed door and secured it with the lock Bob had given him.

"Flimsy lock."

"Ya think?" Howie frowned as he pocketed the key.

"Yeah. Used to break into these in under a minute, in my wild and crazy youth." Moss bent down and tugged at the padlock. "Considering everyone bidding got a look at the gym equipment in there, you might want to get something sturdier, especially if you're going to rent the place."

"Good idea. Thanks."

"Want me to come by tomorrow and give you a hand?"

"Nah. I've got this covered, but if your friend wants the bike let me know."

"I'll do that."

He was late. So like Howie, her recalcitrant son. She'd checked her phone and email a dozen times. Nothing. Text? None. Sara looked away from her phone and down South Henry Street. A sea of people filled her view, mostly tourists waiting in line for outside tables at the restaurants in Merchants Square on this beautiful fall day.

But no sign of Howie.

Sara stood. Time to go. Thirty minutes was more than enough time to wait. She shook her head in disgust, handed the server a ten dollar bill, more than enough to cover her iced tea and the time she occupied the table at The DoG Street Pub, and shouldered her purse.

And repeated the promise she made to herself the last time Howie invited her to lunch then didn't show. She waited a full hour that time. Howie's excuse, when it came, would fall into the "you won't believe what happened, Mom. I couldn't help it. It wasn't my fault" category.

Nothing is ever his fault.

It was almost dark when Sara heard Howie's car pull into the driveway.

"Hey, Mom." He tossed his car keys onto the hall table. "Sorry I missed lunch today. I got caught up talking to this guy who's gonna buy the motorcycle from the shed. He's talking twenty thousand. I couldn't just cut him off."

Howie rocked from foot to foot as he spoke, his eyes shifting from point to point, looking everywhere but at his mom. Small beads of sweat clung to his newly-grown mustache.

And his hands. His hands were giving him trouble. They were all over the place. In his pockets, on his hips, taking his cap off and then putting it back on, tugging at his shirt sleeves, retying his shoelaces.

"Twenty thousand, sight unseen, for a motorcycle?" asked Sara.

"Yeah. He's a collector. Works on 'em. Fixes 'em up."

"And when will this wonderful deal take place?"

"He said he'd get back to me in a few days. He's kinda short on cash right now. Said he just bought a Harley up north."

"And you believe him?"

76

"What's not to believe? At least I'm talking to someone, making a deal. That friend of yours, Moss, hasn't come through with the guy he knows, so I'm making my own plans."

"That's the story you're sticking with?"

"You better believe it."

"And you couldn't put him on hold while you texted me that you weren't coming?"

"Come on, Ma. It was one lunch."

"It was a lunch you invited me to, to make up for the one you missed the other day."

"Tell you what, I'll take you to dinner. How's that?"

Sara threw up her hands. "No need. I've got plans for tonight."

Howie watched his mom touch up her lipstick in the hall mirror.

"There's food in the fridge. But please, if your buyer calls back, don't invite him over here. No strangers in my house."

"Got it. Can't believe you're this pissed because I missed lunch."

"Howie, it's not about lunch. It's about what you're saying and what you're doing." Sara put on a sweater and sighed. "I guess finally, after all these years, I'm sick of your bullshit."

"I'm telling you the truth."

"There's truth," said Sara, leaning forward and touching him gently on the cheek, "and then there's truth. The real truth, and nothing but the truth. The kind you swear to with your hand on the Bible."

"Didn't think they still did that."

"They do. So which truth are you talking?"

Howie started walking down the hall to his bedroom. "Have a nice night. Tell Rachel hello." He slammed the door.

CHAPTER 11

Moss blended into the night, dressed head to toe in black. He'd spent about a half hour talking to the storage facility's owner, pretending to be a potential renter. She was heavy into her sales pitch, boasting about both an alarm system and video surveillance, telling him about the facility's cleanliness, inside and outside units of varying sizes, and twenty-four hour access.

When Moss asked about human security after hours, she indicated the on-site phones were answered immediately by an off-site security company in case someone needed help, and bragged about them never having a single break-in.

Moss breathed a sigh of relief. With twenty-four-hour access, there wouldn't be any guard dogs roaming unrestrained at night. Alarms he could handle, a guard he could subdue, but a German Shepard, or more likely a Belgian Malinois, would cast a different light on his evening's breaking and entering agenda.

He left his car in the parking lot of the Family Inn on Airport Road and hoofed it to the storage facility about a mile down Mooretown Road. Needing freedom of movement, he'd left his sling back in Rachel and Daniel's guest room.

Claiming to have been shot was a good subterfuge, and served its purpose by encouraging certain people to think he was out of commission for a few weeks—which gave him a solid excuse to leave his undercover job on the fishing boat. If the DEA wanted him back in Wachapreague, all he had to do was show up, flex his arm, and show his boss, Yankov, that he was all healed and ready to work.

But current events told him that was not going to happen.

When he got to the storage lot, he walked around the perimeter, doing a quick recon of the facility, testing the strength of the fencing. The place looked deserted, but he knew looks could be deceiving. No lights in the office confirmed there was no night guard, and seeing no cars in any aisles told him no renters were there. More good news was that Howie's unit was outside, at the end of a back row next to the fence, and shielded in semi-darkness.

Howie had said he'd be emptying the unit the next day, and Moss's conversation with the owner alerted him to the video camera locations. With four quick maneuvers he scaled the chain link fence in under thirty seconds. He found unit seventy-five and went to work.

Moss knelt down, pulled his trusty lock pick from its case, and started to pick the cheap padlock, but stopped when he heard a car's engine and saw headlight beams turning toward him from the main aisle.

He backed into the shadows as a small panel van approached. It stopped at unit seventy-five. Two men got out, one fit-looking black guy wearing jeans and a Tupac Shakur T-shirt, the other a muscle-bound white dude dressed all in black. Both looked like they could bench press over two hundred pounds. The white guy opened the side of the van while the other guy pulled something out of his pocket, bent down to the lock, and unlocked the unit. He rolled up the door and they went inside.

Moss had to get closer. Moving stealthily from his position, he crept to the back side of the van, taking the opportunity to photograph the license plate while both men were inside the shed. He ducked back when one man came out, got a portable, battery-powered work light out of the van, and set it up, blasting daylight inside the shed.

"*Êtes-vous sûr de savoir quelles boîtes prendre?*" the larger man asked, questioning how they would know which boxes to take.

"*Oui. Ils sont adressés à Sherlock Holmes.*"

"Sherlock Holmes?" said the larger man in English. "Not very original."

"*C'est ce que c'est.* It is what it is."

In under twenty minutes Moss counted more than fifty cartons had been moved from the storage unit to the van. Whatever was in them was more important than an antique motorcycle. He needed to know who these guys were and where they were going, but his car was too far away, so he couldn't follow them. Only one option available—go with them. Without hesitating, he crept into the van when both men had their backs to him and hid behind the cartons.

"*C'est tout.* Let's go."

The black guy got behind the wheel and started the engine while the other guy locked up the shed, closed the van door, and jumped into the passenger seat.

The van had no windows, so Moss concentrated on the van's turns and the feel of the road. He could hear the automatic gate close behind him when they left the property, and he knew the right turn put them on Mooretown Road heading south. He felt the van navigate a left-leaning curve in the road, then after another right and quick left, he was sure they were on the Route 60 bypass. After a brief stop at what he assumed was a traffic light, he again felt the van veer right, followed by a left. They went about another mile or two and then made a left. Gravel crunched under the van's tires and it came to a stop.

He heard two doors slam and the sound of footsteps squishing gravel, so he knew both men had walked away. He slowly lifted the door handle of the van's back door and slipped out. Spotting trees, he headed for the cover they would provide. Turning around, he saw a lone porch light illuminate a small, dark house behind which was a single car garage backed by woods.

The porch door opened. A short, reed-thin, balding man wearing coke-bottle thick, round wire-framed glasses came out. In the porch light Moss could see his scalp shining through his comb-over.

Now there were three men.

Alone, hidden by the trees, Moss watched and waited. Two men jumped into the van, which started up and drove past the garage and into the woods, toward a lone light shining in the distance. The third lit a cigarette and followed the van down a narrow, dark path.

Moss had to get closer. He carefully slid through the trees, placing each foot slowly on the ground to minimize any sounds. He came upon a second garage after a few minutes and saw the two men had already opened the van doors and were waiting for the third guy to reach them.

"Could you move any slower?"

"What's your rush? It's not like anyone can see us back here. It's just us and the snakes, the birds, an occasional deer, and the bugs. We have all night." The third guy stuck his cigarette butt into an old terra cotta flower pot next to the door, bent down, and, punctuating the strain with a somber grunt, lifted the door. They all got to work unloading the boxes.

Something isn't right, thought Moss. *This second garage is too far from the house, buried in the woods. Why?*

His patience paid off when, an hour later, the van left with the two men and the third locked up the garage and headed back up the path to the house. Within minutes everything went dark, although he could still see the house porch light twinkle in the distance as the wind blew through the trees. Moss walked up the path, waited until he saw the interior house lights go out, and then waited some more to ensure the guy was off to dreamland.

Moss approached the garage with caution, his night-vision equipped Maglite sweeping the ground while he searched for any silent alarm trigger wires that could signal his presence. He snuck around the side looking for other means of egress, and on the side facing the trees he found a side door with a standard Schlage door lockset.

What is it with people and locks? Moss unzipped his Leatherman tool kit and went to work. The door's lock clicked open in under a minute. Child's play.

Moss slipped inside and took out his Maglite, aiming it around the space. There were cartons everywhere, piled high, many more than what was taken from Howie's storage shed. He flipped open his Ka-Bar combat knife and picked at the tape on one box, making sure to lift it carefully, following the best practices of the leave-no-trace philosophy.

Drugs. But not the type he expected. Not weed. Not heroin. Not cocaine. Not oxy. Not fentanyl. The carton contained boxes of amoxicillin. He resealed the carton, moved to the other side of the room, and again carefully opened another carton. Inside he found boxes of aspirin. Inside a third carton, he found his most worrisome surprise, insulin. Vials of insulin stored in a box in a garage that was not temperature-controlled.

He pulled out his cell phone, took photos of the boxes of drugs so he could start a trace of the lot numbers, then texted Daniel. The message said it all. *Saddle up.*

Jesse made Baltimore in just under three hours. His first stop when he reached the Johns Hopkins campus was the bathroom. Then he signed in at the security desk, got his visitor's pass, and headed to the third floor, room three hundred, the office and lab of Dr. Ravinder Patel.

"Ravi, how goes the war? Are we winning yet?"

"Hard to say." Ravi's face was so serious. "Too many variables."

"Spoken like a true scientist." Their handshake evolved into a man hug. "It's been too long," said Jesse. "Sorry I couldn't stay when I dropped off the samples for testing. But today, if you have time, let's get some lunch."

"Sounds good. Give me a few minutes to finish up here. A new micro-brewery opened down the street and they make a great veggie burger."

"You vegan, you. Moo!"

Ten minutes later the friends were comfortably ensconced in a back booth away from prying eyes. The restaurant wasn't crowded, so none of the surrounding tables were occupied.

The server, whose name tag said "Dorie," took their order, both having the Honey Malt Pale Ale, soft pretzels with a red lager cheese sauce and spiced mustard, one stout grilled burger and one stout grilled veggie burger, sweet potato fries, and coleslaw. Dorie took away the menus and returned quickly with their drinks.

"That was fast," said Jesse.

"You both look thirsty. Your pretzels should be out shortly."

"I don't mean to rush you," said Jesse, sipping his beer, "but I gotta know. What did you find when you tested the samples I brought you?"

"In keeping with our brewery surroundings," Ravi held out his hands, "diluted and full-bodied." He looked from his left hand to his right as he made his pronouncements.

"Let me guess," said Jesse. "The one with the silver cap was diluted and the red cap was full-strength, the real deal."

"Exactly. I ran the samples through my trusty mass spectrometer and got their chemical makeup. One was full strength Ciprofloxacin, but the other one was so diluted, it couldn't have cured a hangnail."

"I knew it. Those thieving bastards." Jesse took a huge gulp of his beer. "Damn them all to hell. How could they do it? And why would they?"

Dorie put down a plate of warm, salted, German-style pretzels and Ravi immediately broke off a chunk and dunked it in the cheese sauce.

"These are so good." He wiped his mouth, "Do you know where those pills you swallow every day come from?"

"I don't take pills." Jesse chomped down on a piece of pretzel.

"Not you. The hypothetical you."

"Okay. No, the hypothetical me doesn't know. Probably CVS, Walgreens, Walmart, you know, one of the major chains. I know Morgan takes cholesterol meds, and she orders them from a ninety-day mail order pharmacy."

"But who supplies the pharmacy?" asked Ravi, who then held up his finger to silence the conversation as Dorie approached with lunch and beer refills. "Let me know if I can get you guys anything else."

"The drug company supplies the pharmacy," said Jesse when they were alone.

"You're thinking like Merck? Or Pfizer? or Novartis? or Johnson & Johnson?"

"Yes. They're big pharma."

"Hate to burst your bubble, but probably not." Ravi's response reverberated in Jesse's brain. "Pharmaceuticals are a commodity, like corn, wheat or pork bellies. Gone are the days of vertical integration, the same company doing everything. Now, a manufacturer orders the API—"

"API?"

"Active Pharmaceutical Ingredient. The chemical that makes the medicine work."

"Okay. Got it."

"The manufacturer orders the API from China—"

"Everything's cheaper in China." Jesse bit into his burger and licked sauce off his fingers.

"Right. The API gets delivered to, say, India, or the Czech Republic, or Ireland—any number of places—where excipients are added—"

"Excipients?"

"The inactive ingredients, which is another scary aspect of all this that I won't get into now. The mix is then sent somewhere else in a fifty-five gallon drum to be pressed into pills, made into capsules, or some other delivery mechanism, and then shipped out to sell."

"If it's a commodity, we're talking price?"

"Yes, and the lowest price wins the sale. There's a huge, tiered network of wholesalers and distributors. Ninety-plus percent of our meds get passed from one wholesaler to the next in the supply chain. And there are smaller distributors along the way. At any point a medicine could be stored improperly or mishandled, which impacts its efficacy."

"And the patient never knows."

"That's right. Probably never gives it a thought."

"Lives depend on the integrity of the drug supply that

everyday people take. We're talking antibiotics, statins, blood thinners, insulin, asthma meds, HIV and cancer drugs, all the way down to aspirin. Who's minding the store?"

"In the US, the FDA. Understaffed and overworked. Keep in mind, too, that FDA approval doesn't always mean the product is safe. Think tobacco. We know it's not a safe product, but the manufacturers complied with all required procedures under the law to bring the product to market, and look how that turned out."

"I think I'm going to be sick."

"I'd stay as healthy as I possibly could if I were you. There are protections in place. Licensing, inspections, sign-offs, but any slip up along the way has catastrophe written all over it."

"And if I remember my Economics 101, every time the meds pass through another middleman, the price increases."

"Yep. Everyone, at every level, is out to make a profit. No one does nothing for free." Ravi wiped his mouth. "Hope your burger is as good as my veggie burger."

"Everyone is screaming for the government to take over health care." Jesse waved a sweet potato fry. "But we know once the government gets its meathooks into an industry, all bets are off. Bribes, looking the other way, you name it— nothing is beyond our faithful bureaucrats' abilities to rip off the general public, all the while proclaiming they're only doing it to protect the people."

"Amen, brother. It's why I wanted you to drive up here, meet you face-to-face, away from prying eyes and ears." Ravi reached across the table and touched Jesse's hand. "I can't do anything about any of this. I'm not the whistleblower type. But you can. Jesse, this story is right up your alley. It could get you that Pulitzer you're drooling over. You need to hit the internet. Based on the articles coming across my desk over the past several years, people are assuming what they get from any of the big chains is safe and coming directly from the well-known manufacturer, but that may not be the case. The pharmaceutical supply chain scares the shit out of me. Manufacturing even more so."

"You're kidding."

Ravi took the last bite of his burger. "I'm on heart meds, and every time I refill my prescriptions I look at the pills and wonder what's really in them. So I crush one and run it through the mass-spec to check out how close the chemical make-up is to what it should be."

"Now you're scaring me, and I don't take any meds."

"Good. You need to be scared. And so does everyone who takes medications. Pull out your phone." Jesse did as he was told. "Google it. Put in counterfeit drugs, fraudulent drugs, fake drugs, black market drugs. Any of those search terms will work."

Jesse's thumbs whipped over the keys and he watched article after article pop up on the phone's small screen.

"How is this possible?"

"Greedy people exploiting loopholes and cashing in on a very lucrative and somewhat unregulated market."

"But the FDA regulates the pharmaceutical industry."

"Here, maybe. But as I said, they're understaffed and overworked, and racing like crazy to investigate what's happening locally."

"Is the recent Zantac recall part of this?"

"Probably. And overseas it's the wild, wild west. Nothing is as it seems. As I said before, eighty to ninety percent of the active ingredients in all medications, regardless of the big pharma name, are coming from China, and manufacturers don't have to report country of origin, just the last place the pill was manufactured. So even if you try, you can't really find out where your pills are coming from."

Jesse finished his burger, threw his napkin on his plate,

and leaned forward. "I sense you have more to say. Enlighten me."

"Some powerful players are upset that China is challenging America's competitive position in the biopharma industry. And other powerful players see pharmaceuticals as a weak link in America's future."

"I never really thought about it in that context. Until Marcel died and I brought you those vials to test, I hadn't considered the ramifications of outsourcing pharmaceutical manufacturing to China or demanding lower drug prices."

"Well, you better gear up, because we are in an all-out war with China over most, if not all, of the medications Americans take every day. And the Chinese are nothing if not a patient people. This is a war they plan to win. Ever hear of the Made in China 2025 plan?"

"No. But I think I'm about to."

"China's goal is to topple the US and become the high-tech global superpower, and to do that the Chinese government knows it must switch from low wage manufacturing like making toys and cheap clothing to advanced technology."

"Sounds like the paradigm shift Japan undertook in the fifties."

"Exactly."

"I know about technology transfer, and intellectual property theft runs rampant. And the Chinese are huge players in cyber espionage. Politicians have been screaming Russia, Russia, Russia, but no one is watching the Chinese. They're cleaning our clocks. I think that's why Trump is being such a hard-ass about tariffs."

Ravi threw up his hands and leaned back in the booth. "The difference between a businessperson and a self-serving politician in the presidency."

"Can I get you anything else?" asked Dorie when she approached the table. "Another beer? Dessert, perhaps?"

"No. Just the check, please," said Jesse.

"Your bill's been taken care of."

Jesse and Ravi exchanged glances. "It has?" asked Jesse. "By whom?"

"I'm not sure. Brian, the shift manager, told me a few minutes ago."

"Could you send him over please?"

A tall, thin guy who barely looked old enough to shave came to the table a few minutes later.

"Is there a problem, Mr. Sinclair?"

"How do you know my name?"

"The gentleman who paid your tab referred to you by name when he pointed to this table."

"What did he look like? Height? Weight?" Jesse thought for a moment. "Skin color?"

"Tall. Thin. Very distinguished-looking. Spoke with an accent." Brian scratched his head. "Is everything okay? I assumed he knew you."

"What made you think that?"

"Well, a guy might buy a stranger a beer if they're sitting next to each other at the bar and strike up a conversation, but not too many people pay the bill for people they don't know. At least that's been my experience."

"Did he happen to use a credit card?"

"Nope. Cash all the way. He even included a really generous tip for Dorie." Brian waited a second for any response. "If there's nothing else, gentlemen, I've got to get back to work."

"Thanks."

They waited until Brian was out of hearing range. "Odd," said Ravi. "Who knew you were coming up here?"

"No one."

Ravi looked at his watch. "I've got to get back."

"I'll come with you so I can get the vials."

"But they're empty."

"You used all of the drugs?" Jesse bowed his head. Rage filled him. The two vials he'd smuggled out of the Congo were empty, their contents used up in testing.

"Didn't think it would be a problem."

"Do you still have the vials?"

"Yes. Back at the lab."

"Okay. I'll take those back. Maybe I can trace their origins from something on the label."

"Doubt it, but knock yourself out."

CHAPTER 12

Sara's grip on her coffee cup tightened when she heard rapping at her kitchen door. She relaxed when she saw a familiar face.

"Hey, Sara."

"Moss, what are you doing here so early? Sundays are for sleeping late." She stepped aside to let him in. "Can I get you some coffee?"

"Sorry about the time, but this can't wait." He dropped his backpack on the floor. "Is Howie home?"

"No. And I haven't got a clue where he is."

"Do you have any idea what Howie's up to?"

She closed the door when he came inside. Looking at his stealthy attire, and considering the early hour, she sensed he'd been up all night and could use breakfast. "I've got eggs and bacon if you're hungry."

"Sounds good, but don't go to any trouble."

"No trouble at all. You can eat and tell me what's got you playing commando at five-thirty in the morning."

He looked at his clothes and picked up his backpack. "Mind if I wash up?"

"Bathroom's that away. Towels are clean if you want to shower."

Ten minutes later he was back, wearing an unbuttoned blue checked shirt and clean jeans. Six-pack abs peeked out from the shirt and rippled in the morning light streaming through the kitchen window.

Sara froze, the coffee pot in her hand, mesmerized by his smile, all dazzling white, straight teeth flashing from honey-mocha skin. She took a deep, careful breath.

"Wow," she said breathlessly, putting the coffee pot down. "You are one put-together man." Without stopping to think or reason, Sara went to him and danced her fingers through soft tufts of curly brown chest hair. "Ya gotta love a man who carries his wardrobe around with him."

"I've always been into older women." His arms encircled her.

"Watch that older stuff."

His lips found hers.

"You sure you want to make breakfast?"

"Rip-your-clothes-off sex sounds better than bacon and eggs to me." Sara blushed at her brazenness. "Fewer calories."

Moss pulled Sara close. This wasn't why he'd come to see her, but the spark had been there since he first met her, intensifying with every encounter.

"Are you sure this is a good idea?"

"Probably not. But who cares?"

He leaned in and brushed her lower lip with his thumb, planted soft kisses on her eyelids. She trembled, and he felt an urging in his loins. Being this close to her, breathing in her scent, every fiber of his being wanted to carry her into her bedroom and make mad, passionate love until the rooster crowed.

"Could really complicate things."

"How so? We're two consenting adults."

"We don't know where this is going. How it's going to end."

"Who said anything about ending? We're just beginning."

"But the age difference?"

"I don't care if you don't care." Moss took a step back. "You know who I am and you know what I do. There is no happily ever after with me. If you're okay with that, then what's to stop us from enjoying each other's company?"

"Nothing… Absolutely nothing."

He scooped her into his arms. "Which way, m'lady?"

"There." She pointed to the bedroom as she pulled out the scrunchie and let her hair fall in waves around her face.

"So pretty."

"Thank you."

And then they were in her bedroom, and his fingers were combing through her hair, coming together on her neck, pulling her to him. His mouth found hers. Hungrily he tasted her. And hungrily she responded.

He nibbled her earlobe lost in a mix of vanilla, rose and jasmine. Their tongues jousted: forward, retreat.

She traced her hands over broad shoulders that narrowed to a V at his waist, then pushed his shirt off his shoulders, down his arms, playing with the brown hairs which curled down his chest, meeting his belt buckle and dipping into his low-riding briefs, exposing a distinctive tan line on his mocha skin. Exploring more aggressively, she ran her hands over his six-pack abs. Hard as granite, strong as steel—a mighty combination.

"Turnabout is fair play." Moss tugged her robe off her shoulders and let it drop to the floor. Her breasts, soft globes of sweet skin, beckoned him, enticed him, commanded his full attention. He pulled her to him and she melted against his chest.

Soft, full, his lips found one nipple and suckled greedily while his hand cupped the other, his thumb rubbing the nipple. Each one hardened and rose to attention under his touch.

"Sorry I didn't make the bed."

"Wasted action since we're going to mess it up big time." With that he lifted her up and gently laid her on the bed.

Hot lips moved back to hers as her body arched against his, enjoying the heat of him, the weight of him on top of her. His hand slid between her legs, two fingers gliding inside her, stroking her, finding her sweet spot, working it, and unleashing a moan and shudder from the top of her head to the tips of her toes.

And then he was inside her, all of him, filling her to bursting.

"Oh!"

"You okay?"

"Yessss."

They moved as one, his thrusts deeper and deeper, sending her further and further over the edge.

An hour later Sara woke up in the crook of Moss's arm, smiling. She looked up at him, still sleeping, with a contented smile on his face. He had rocked her world twice while the sun crested the trees and peeked into the bedroom, announcing morning's arrival. Now he was sleeping like a baby.

She wondered what had prompted the early morning visit, knew it had something to do with Howie, and sighed. For these few brief moments before the shit hit the fan, she was content to wallow in the afterglow of love well made.

"To answer your question," said Sara, when they reconvened in the kitchen with bacon and eggs steaming on their plates, "I haven't a clue what Howie's really into, but knowing him, it can't be good." Sara took a sip of coffee. "Do we have to talk about Howie?"

"Kind of. He bought a storage shed yesterday, but his rush to leave before checking out all its contents got me curious. Made an unannounced trip last night. Wanted to get a peek inside, but some guys in a van pulled up, emptied out some boxes, and hauled them away."

"Shit." Sara ran her fingers through her hair. "That boy is always in trouble."

"This trouble may be more than he bargained for."

"It always is."

A resigned silence took over as they both dug into breakfast. Finally Moss took a break, wiping his mouth.

"Penny for your thoughts."

"Save your money."

"It can't be that bad."

"My son sells drugs. Not a doctor. Not a lawyer. A drug dealer. Every Jewish mother's dream."

"You're being too hard on yourself. Once they leave the nest, you can only hope for the best, and even then it's a crap shoot."

"You can say that again."

"What does Howie do for money? Drugs cost. How does he pay for his stuff?"

"I don't know. Occasionally he hits me up. Says it's for rent or a car payment, but he mostly crashes with friends or stays at fleabag motels. And he doesn't own a car. When he needs one, he rents it."

"Needing money is a powerful motivator."

"Tell me about it. I married my first husband for his money. Instead I got a man who couldn't boil water, take out the trash, or put a damn dirty mug in the dishwasher."

"I followed the guys to a house on the other side of town." Moss refreshed both mugs with coffee, finished his eggs, and took his plate to the sink. "Daniel and I are meeting this morning to talk about what I found."

"What can I do?" Sara cleared the rest of the table.

"Do you know where he is?"

"Nope. I found dirty clothes on the floor in his room and wet towels hung over the shower rod, so I know he was here for a while. I hate to say it, but he's probably off getting high somewhere."

"I'm so sorry." He took her in his arms. "I want to help if I can."

"That's sweet of you." Sara tried to swallow past the lump in her throat. "Howie was always a sensitive kid. Having an uncaring bastard for a father didn't help. My second husband, Marv, tried to connect with him, but it was too late. Howie was already into weed and God knows what else. I got him help, but it didn't help."

"He has to want help. Without that, help never works."

"You speaking from experience?"

"Not me personally, but I know a lot of guys who got strung out. Some made it back. Too many didn't."

"Howie's always got an angle, a scheme, a way to get rich, but they never work out. And I'm guessing this one… buying storage sheds and selling whatever he finds inside… won't either. And he'll start using again. It's a vicious cycle. I'm at my wits' end."

"It's hard to watch someone you love killing themselves with drugs."

"Very painful. I feel helpless."

"Maybe I can help."

"How?"

"Not sure, but I'm willing to give it a try."

"Thanks. Anything you can do, I'll support."

❖

Debra McKenna knocked on the metal screen door and waited. This was one house call she was excited about making.

"Why, hello doctor…doctor…"

"McKenna," Debra said. "I took care of Lette in the ER last week."

"Yes. I remember you, I'm not very good with names is all. Come in."

Mrs. Lee opened the screen door and stood to the side as Debra entered.

"You'll have to excuse the place. I wasn' 'spectin' company and we just got back from church. Lette's in her room. Lemme call her."

"That would be great. I apologize for not calling." Debra put her medical bag down on a small table in the entranceway and looked around. Just as Burt, the van driver who brought them home, had said, the place was super-neat and clean.

"Wouldn' have mattered if you did. My phone's outta minutes and I gotta wait till I get paid to get more."

Lette appeared in the hallway, hugging the wall, her eyes cast down at the floor.

"Come here, child. Look who's come to visit." Mrs. Lee waved Lette over. "Can I get you something to drink? Some coffee?"

"No. Nothing for me." Debra turned her attention to the little girl. "How are you feeling, Lette?"

"Fine." Her voice barely above a whisper, Lette backed away.

"That's good," said Dr. McKenna, while she reached inside her bag and pulled out her stethoscope. "Would it be okay with you, Lette, if I check you over? Just to be sure everything is working like it should?"

Still not making eye contact, the little girl nodded consent. Dr. McKenna put in the eartips and listened to the little girl's heart. "Take a few deep breaths for me." She listened intently, moving the chest piece from front to back. "Would you like to listen?"

The question brought a smile to Lette's face.

Debra dug into her bag and found fresh eartips, then explained to Mrs. Lee, "I always carry extra because I find children are excited when they hear the sound of their own hearts." She quickly replaced the eartips and placed them in the child's ears. Then she put the chest piece over the girl's heart.

Thump-thump...thump-thump...thump-thump.

Lette's eyes popped wide when she heard the beats of her heart. Debra could see the tension melt from the little girl's body. *Now for the hard part.*

"Lette, is it okay if I test the sugar level in your blood?" Debra held the small lancet up. "It will be a little ouch on your finger. Then I'll put a drop of your blood on this test strip. And we can see the results together."

Reluctantly, Lette put out her hand.

"Mrs. Lee, when was the last time Lette ate?"

"This mornin'. I was just about to start lunch when you knocked."

"Great. I just need that information to accurately assess Lette's insulin levels."

In under a minute the test was done.

"Looks good," said Dr. McKenna. "I can see you've been taking your insulin, and I am so proud of you." Turning to Mrs. Lee, Debra said, "Thank you for your hospitality. I've brought you some additional insulin for Lette."

Mrs. Lee accepted the cold-pack-wrapped package from Dr. McKenna.

"I can't thank you enough for your kindness. The people at the Sentara clinic has been so nice to us." Mrs. Lee started for the door, then stopped. A serious expression took over her face. "Did ya catch him?"

"Who?"

"The man who sold me the bad insulin. Did ya get him?"

"No. Not yet. Detective Knight is working on it, though, and I'm sure he'll make an arrest soon."

"That's good. I know I shouldn't think this way. It ain' Christian and all, but he needs to pay for what he did to my Lette. I was gonna go back to the flea market and give him a piece of my mind, but—"

"You leave that to Detective Knight. He's very good at what he does, and I'm sure he'll be in touch if and when he needs you to make a positive identification."

CHAPTER 13

When Jesse walked into Morgan's home office holding a huge blue can of Planter's peanuts and started to talk, she held up her finger, signaling him to wait. He hadn't noticed she was on the phone.

"But, Tiffany, why can't you tell me?" she asked the person on the other end of the line. "It's a simple question. Where was the Ciprofloxacin manufactured? There are fifty states. Pick one."

Morgan wiggled her head, nodded, and dipped as she listened to the response. "I'm sorry. I'm not trying to be difficult, but you must have records."

More listening and frowning on Morgan's part had Jesse's ears perking up.

"Oh?" Morgan shot Jesse a glance. "In that case, can I talk to your supervisor? Or is there someone else there who might know the answer to my question?"

"In a meeting. I see. When will he be available?"

"Okay. I'll call back tomorrow. Tiffany, thank you so much for your help." She hung up, rubbed her hands over her face and collapsed back in her chair, exasperated.

"Doesn't sound like you got very far," said Jesse.

"It's been frustrating, to say the least. And Tiffany told me more than the other people I spoke to today."

"Like what?"

"That, and I quote, her company has a highly evolved and complex supply chain, spanning several countries, with different suppliers fulfilling different aspects of any given drug's manufacturing process."

"That sounds like gobbledygook."

Morgan flipped a page on the yellow pad in front of her. "I love this one. 'We source our ingredients from multiple suppliers, always looking for the best price to ensure that we can offer consumers the lowest price possible for any given pharmaceutical.'"

"Best price, my ass. It's more like 'How high can we set our price?' That's what big pharma is doing. They make huge profits by ripping off people who need their meds to stay alive."

"Your cynical side is showing." Morgan put a handful of peanuts into her mouth. "Hard to believe someone could die from what I just ate." She took another handful. "This investigative reporter thing isn't easy. Maybe I should go back to writing obituaries and garden club news."

"Nothing important is easy, and what we're doing is very important. Besides, you hated your job. If I remember correctly, you begged me to take you on, show you how investigative journalism sausage really gets made."

"I'm not sure about the begging part, but I imagined more glamorous settings, not being stuck making phone calls from the confines of my home office." She waved her hands around the room. "You're the one getting the glamorous travel."

"Sub-Saharan Africa isn't my idea of glamorous travel. Two months without a good, hot shower or a decent meal, and bugs the size of my fist, wasn't fun."

"You were kind of odoriferous when you finally got here." Morgan got up, pulled a bottle of water and a bottle of beer out of the mini fridge, handed the beer to Jesse and gave him a kiss as she passed by.

"Did you learn anything new?"

"Only that no one wants to talk to me. Manufacturing locations are a bigger secret than the Manhattan Project was. Wonder why?"

"Because what the consumer doesn't know can't lead to any lawsuits should something go wrong."

"I'd ask what could go wrong, but we've already uncovered cases where things went terribly wrong and people died." Morgan rifled through her notes. "Contaminated heparin killed over eighty people in 2008. Levermir insulin problems in 2009. Over sixty dead in twenty states from a fungal meningitis outbreak in 2012. And my gut's telling me there are many more I haven't found yet."

"I'm going out for a while. Have to meet a man about a horse."

"Can I come?"

"Nope. Don't want to spook the guy. But I'll have my recorder on so you can hear what went down when I get back."

Turning the corner off Scotland Street, Jesse found himself face-to-face with a reed-thin black kid concealing the business end of a gun in the sleeve of his oversized hoodie.

Shit. I'm getting mugged in broad daylight in downtown Williamsburg, a block away from William and Mary. Jesse put his hands out in front of him, but not up in surrender. His eyes never left his would-be assailant.

"You don't want to do this, man." Jesse took a step, closing the distance between himself and the kid. If he reached out he could touch him, but the stupid kid didn't back away.

"Got to. Wallet. Gimme it. Now." The kid had his jeans slung low, a belt strategically cinched at his hip bones to keep them from falling off. Blue striped boxers filled the space between hips and waist. The gun, held sideways like you see druggies do on TV, shook in the kid's hands.

"Let me help you," said Jesse, his hands still out in front of him. He adjusted his stance, feet slightly wider than his hips, knees aligned with his feet, abs taut, weight evenly distributed.

"You are, man. Money." The kid wiggled his fingers at Jesse. "Now. And your backpack. Give me that too."

Jesse's lightning fast jab to the guy's Adam's apple forced him to drop the gun as he reached for his throat and doubled over in pain. Following the jab with a swift kick to the assailant's groin, Jesse then twisted him around and put him down to the ground with a knee planted firmly in the guy's back. Then he reached out and shoved the gun out of reach.

"Whaaaat."

"I warned you."

Jesse pulled out his cell, hit 911, and dragged the guy to his feet.

"Come on. Let's get you some help."

Pfft. Pfft.

The staccato sound of shots fired had Jesse diving down and hugging the sidewalk. As soon as he released his grip on his assailant, the guy grabbed his gun and bolted. Jesse looked up to see him jump into the back of a black SUV, which hit the gas and careened down North Boundary Street, made a right onto Lafayette, and was quickly out of sight.

Two police officers arrived a few minutes later to find Jesse sitting on a bench outside the library. He'd called them back and told them the kid who assaulted him bolted, but they still sent a car.

"You didn't get a look at the car's driver?" asked one officer.

"Nope. I heard shots, hit the ground, and the next thing I knew the kid was jumping into the SUV and they were gone."

"No plate number?"

"Couldn't see it from my vantage point kissing the sidewalk." Jesse looked around and pointed at the Stryker building, "Any cameras over there?"

"We'll check."

"They made a right on Lafayette," Jesse pointed toward the corner. "Think the light might have been red when they went through it, so if there's a camera on that corner, you could get lucky and get a plate number."

The officer made some notes. "You said he wanted your wallet and your money, but now you think something different?"

"Yeah. I think the money part of the robbery was fake. He wanted my backpack."

"Why would he want that?"

"Because maybe he thought I had something in it that was more valuable than money."

The two officers exchanged glances. "And what might that be?"

"Don't know, but I'm going to find out." Jesse got up and looked around. "Thanks for coming out. There's not much more I can say. Let's just drop it."

"Can't really drop it if you heard gunshots like you claim."

"I'm sure I was mistaken. Maybe a car revving up…or a motorcycle backfiring. I remember one did go down the street while this was happening. Let's chalk it up to a case of nerves."

"Nerves?" said one officer. "You managed to subdue a guy holding a gun on you, but now you're claiming nerves? I'd say that was pretty gutsy."

"I call it stupidly overconfident after a few martial arts lessons. I'm sorry I've taken up your time." Jesse shook both officers' hands. "It all happened so fast. The guy didn't get any money, and I think I scared him with my kung fu ninja moves, so I'm sure he'll think twice before he tries to mug anyone else. Thanks for coming out. Really. Thank you."

Jesse left the two officers and headed up Scotland Street to his parked car. He could feel their eyes on him, but he knew he'd said too much already. He got into his car, started the engine, and pulled out, heading toward Richmond Road.

A hand threaded into the crook of Moss's arm as he walked through the lobby of the Williamsburg Inn. The cryptic text simply stated today's date, a time, and the place. A familiar scent foretold whose face he would see when he turned around—and stopped him from taking more aggressive action.

"Moss, my love, might we have a word?"

"Soraya." A wary look crossed his face. "It's been a long time."

"Too long," she said, extending her manicured hand to touch his cheek. "Shall we renew our acquaintance over a beverage?"

"Why?"

"Why what? Why share a libation? Or why have a few words?"

"Both."

"Indulge me. A drink because it's the sociable thing to do with an old friend you haven't seen in a long time. A few words because…well, what I have to say may prove interesting to you."

Moss followed Soraya to an empty table in a more secluded area of the cafe. He ogled her slender figure, beautifully revealed in a muted red sheath dress, stiletto heels, shiny black hair falling halfway down her back. Huge diamond studs glinted on her earlobes, and ruby red lips accentuated every word. His eyes darted around the room, noting other men falling under Soraya's spell.

"How have you been, darling?" she asked after their martinis arrived.

"Let's cut the crap, shall we? I'm not your darling and we're not friends. I'm here because your text invitation was intriguing. Say what you want to say and I'll be on my way."

"Such haste. It's a beautiful day. What's your hurry?"

"Did you ever hear the saying, 'time is what life is made up of'?"

Soraya nodded. "And Confucius said, 'It does not matter how slowly you go as long as you do not stop.' Let's relax, enjoy our drinks, catch up with each other."

"We're on my time now, and I don't choose to waste it talking to you."

"Yet you wasted a good portion of your life serving our mutual friend Hayden. How is he, anyway?"

"Dead. I'm surprised you don't know that. But you probably do. You always did prefer slinking around, playing mind games."

"Ah. Mind games. The battle of the sexes." She leaned forward and touched his hand. "Do you know what I'm thinking now?"

"Can't begin to imagine. Flunked Wizardry 101. The thoughts that go on in a woman's mind…much less your mind. Let's just say I'm smart enough not to even try to assume I could figure out what you or any woman is thinking at any given point in time."

"Very funny."

"I'm serious. Kind of like that movie *What Women Want*. Only I didn't fall into a bathtub full of water and get zapped by a hair dryer. So tell me, what are you thinking?"

The server brought a small plate of olives, tapenade, and toast points to the table. Soraya reached for a toast point, spread the rich tapenade on it and handed it to Moss.

"I have a proposition for you. One that might prove quite lucrative."

"I'm fine right now." Moss accepted the hors d'oeuvre and popped it in his mouth.

"Are you really?" Her arched eyebrow punctuated her doubt. "Fine, that is? What did Hayden pay you for your servitude? A mere pittance in light of what a man like you, with your skills, is worth, I suspect." Soraya reached across the table, covering Moss's hand with her own. "He always took advantage of you. He took your loyalty for granted. You've more than paid any debt...real or perceived. It was a long time ago. You were kids. Why did you do it?"

"It's complicated." Moss watched her every move, every nuance, looking for a clue to inform his side of this awkward conversation. *What the hell does she want?*

Eyeing him over the rim of her martini glass, Soraya calculated her every move, nothing done in haste, no movement without purpose.

"Complications can tax one's systems." She smiled and raised her glass. "To your continued good health."

Moss mimicked the move with an empty hand. "And to yours. Stay out of my business and it will be assuredly so. Are we done here, or are you ready to tell me the reason behind your text?"

Soraya gave him a sly grin and put her glass on the table.

"Down to business, I see. Very well. I have a proposition for you. An interesting and very lucrative avenue of operation has presented itself to me, one that requires the assistance of someone with your unique and varied skills. You'll be handsomely paid." Soraya's mouth curled into an inviting smile.

"Money isn't everything. There are some things more important than money."

"Spare me the God, country, family, honor crap." She plucked an olive from the little dish of treats. "You're talking to me, remember? I was there. I watched. I know what you've done for king and country, and honor wasn't even a thought in that twisted mind of yours. What I'm asking is a cakewalk compared to your antics in Somalia."

"That was then. Under orders. This is now. Besides, I don't trust you."

"And you trusted them? Your generals? You have been told more lies by your precious CIA than there's tea in China." Soraya laughed at the irony of discussing this business right under the CIA's nose, at the Williamsburg Inn, in the backyard of the vaunted CIA training facility, Camp Peary, better known as The Farm.

Moss started to rise. "I don't work for drug dealers."

"Wait, please. I'm not talking about drugs." She sipped her martini. "Well, not narcotics." She took a moment to spread another toast point with tapenade and take a bite. "There's a whole new opportunity that is proving more profitable and less risky. And in some ways my new venture is actually government-sanctioned. Or at least at this point, the government can't get its arms around it."

"Speaking of points, why don't you get to yours." Moss sat back down. "Vagueness doesn't become you."

"I've been approached by some new friends who want me to join them in an international pharmaceutical venture.

It would be a fifty-fifty split, and I'd be willing to share my fifty percent equally with you...considering your unique talents."

"How very generous of you."

"Do you know much about pharmaceuticals?"

"That's a big knowledge category. Care to narrow it down a bit?"

"Manufacturing and distribution?"

"Most meds are easy to manufacture. Only need the chemical ingredients, a pill press, and some small plastic bags. Distribution takes care of itself. All that's required is a prescription by a certified doctor or nurse practitioner. And there are ways around that too."

"Yes. But I'm not talking about the mundane, small time, day-to-day machinations of some pill pusher."

"Then what?"

"Think bigger." Her hands flew up in an imaginary, all-encompassing circle. "More expansive. Name a disease and list all the meds associated with it. Imagine being able to tap into all legitimate pharmaceuticals at the supply level. There is a great deal of money to be made from big pharma, an industry that has a viselike grip on the lives of so many politicians that few can resist doing its bidding."

"You've lost me."

"Big Pharma. Legal pharmaceuticals. Medications advertised on television to the general public with the 'ask your doctor' call to action. Did you know only America and New Zealand allow direct to consumer advertising for pharmaceuticals?"

"No. I didn't know that."

"Pharmaceutical companies have made millions... billions...and my associates have found a way to tap into that lucrative market."

"Sounds illegal to me."

"Not really. We simply manipulate the supply chain, the who, what, and where various medications are manufactured. Controlling the supply chain gives us huge opportunities for profits."

"Why do you need me?"

"Security, of course. It's your wheelhouse, what you do best. Occasionally there are problems which are beyond our control. We're experiencing one of these situations now, as a matter of fact. Here in Williamsburg, no less. And when I learned you were in the area, I knew you were the right person to handle our…situation."

So many bells and whistles were exploding in Moss's head he could barely concentrate on what Soraya was saying.

"How's the arm, by the way? I notice you aren't wearing the sling today. Are you all healed?"

"The arm's fine. Could you be a little more specific? What has happened in your operation that requires my services?"

"All in good time." Soraya finished her drink and stood. "For now, all I need to know is whether you're interested."

"Soraya, our history is not exactly one that affords me the ability to trust you. I need more solid information before I can commit to anything. Perhaps a meeting with your partners is in order."

"Let me discuss it with them. I'll text you."

Soraya picked up her clutch purse and left Moss at the table, sashaying out with a dozen eyes following her every move.

Whether Moss decided to join her was immaterial. His presence told her all she needed to know. He was curious, interested. Moss, the disruptor, had derailed previous contracts, forcing her to alter her plans, backtrack on commitments, and permanently remove potential obstacles before their interference caused irreversible problems.

But having Moss the disruptor working for her changed everything. And for that, she'd pay handsomely.

"Answer my phone please, Jesse," said Morgan, since her hands were elbow-deep in soapy water.

A garbled voice spewed obscenities.

"Who is this?" barked Jesse.

Nothing.

"Who was that?"

"Don't know. The line went dead fast, like as soon as whoever it was realized he didn't get you." His stern expression broadcast a mix of anger and concern as he stared at Morgan. "Who was that?"

"I don't know."

"How many of these calls have you gotten?" Jesse could feel acid reflux filling his throat.

"A few."

"What's a few? Give me a number."

"Maybe five, give or take."

Morgan dried her hands and then started drying the big spaghetti pot. "They started right after we sent in the story idea to the Herald editor. You were up in Baltimore so you weren't here to notice. I take it you haven't gotten any."

"They probably assume it'll be easier to scare you than me."

"I was going to tell you."

"When?" He'd been on the receiving end of death threats ever since his first exposé on rat-infested inner city schools, calling out politicians to put some money and muscle behind their fake concern about poor children. But this was different. The target was Morgan.

"I don't know. Freaked me out at first, but when nothing happened... Can we just drop it?"

"No, we can't just drop it. I couldn't tell whether it was a male or female voice. Whoever it is must be using one of those distorters. What does the caller say?"

"Usual threats. What they're going to do to me. They've never actually mentioned the story we're investigating, so I've been chalking it up to kids pranking me."

"Why you? Why would kids be pranking you?" Jesse could barely swallow. His throat felt like a vise was clamped around his neck.

"Don't know. And no, I haven't pissed anyone off lately. Not more than usual, anyway." She put the colander insert back into the dried pot and set both on the stove. "I don't know if it's connected, but a few days ago, when I was visiting friends at the Beacon, Kevin in the mailroom told me he chased away a guy in the parking lot who was taking pictures of my car.

A heavy silence filled the kitchen. Jesse opened his arms and pulled Morgan into them.

"I'm sorry. I...I don't want anything to happen to you. Why didn't you tell me?"

"I didn't want you to worry about me. I'm an investigative reporter working on a story. Period. I have to be able to accept the accolades my story generates as well as the assholes."

"Come with me." He led her to the bedroom and dug into his backpack. His hand emerged cradling a gun.

"What's that?" Her eyes opened wide.

Jesse cocked his head. "Have you ever fired a gun?"

"No. Never even held one. I believe the pen is mightier than the sword. It's why I became a journalist."

"If someone is trying to kill you, a pen is a pretty useless weapon." He pulled back the slide to rack a bullet and handed her the gun.

"It's heavy."

112

"It's loaded. One in the chamber. Ten in the magazine. Just flick the safety here, point and shoot. Aim for center mass. You may not kill whoever it is, but you'll definitely slow 'em down."

CHAPTER 14

"Care to take a ride to Lowe's?" Jesse telegraphed a message with his eyes that Daniel found intriguing.

"Sure." He stuck his head out to the deck, where Rachel, Morgan, and Sara were engaged in yet another mah jongg game. "Rachel, Jesse and I are heading for Lowe's. Do you need me to stop for anything?"

"Ah, boy shopping. Nope, don't need anything. Have fun."

Daniel followed Jesse out to his car, got in the passenger seat and smiled. His curiosity went into overdrive when Jesse turned onto Monticello but didn't take the ramp onto Route 199.

"Okay, what gives? This is not the way to Lowe's. Care to tell me where we're going?"

"Library."

"Because?"

"Two reasons. First, last night, after dinner, Morgan admitted that she's been getting threatening phone calls."

"Did she call the police?"

"No. So far her response has been to ignore them. She's chalking it up to kids."

"Morgan doesn't know any kids."

"I know."

"Not my first choice," said Daniel. "I've got a friend who may be able to shed some light on where they're coming from." Daniel pulled out his cell. "Before I text him, what's the second reason?"

"You can't breathe a word of this to Morgan. Yesterday, when I was supposed to be running errands, I thought I was meeting a source. A kid with a gun showed up instead. I took him down, but before I could get anything out of him, someone took a shot at me."

"What? Someone shot at you? Did you call it in?"

"Yeah. I told the officers who showed up that some guy tried to mug me. The getting shot at part I fudged over. But I'm hoping you can help me find the bullets."

"Bullets?"

"I think there were two shots. I'm hoping the slugs are lodged in the side of the library building."

"Jeez, Jesse. Shots fired. What did you tell the cops?"

"That I was mistaken. Was a motorcycle backfiring. Scared me because of the mugging."

"You lied."

"Sue me." Jesse bounced his hands off the steering wheel. He got lucky when he pulled into the library parking lot and found a space. "I get it if you don't want to help me, but you've got more experience investigating crime scenes, and because other than a hole in the wall, I'm not sure what to look for."

"Come on. Show me where you were standing."

They walked through the parking lot to North Boundary Street, made a right, and went halfway down the block.

"I was around here." Jesse took up a position with his back to the building. "I swear I felt the bullet whiz by me, so the only place the slug could be is in the building."

Daniel looked up and down the street. Facing out, most of the structures were two-story houses. The tallest structure was the parking garage on North Henry Street, kitty-corner to where they were, but about a block away.

"Okay. Let's get started."

They backed up to the library's wall. A three-foot-high row of hedges fronted the building.

"How tall are you?"

"Almost six feet."

"Okay. I'm guessing close to the ground might be the best place to look, but we don't know anything about the skill of the shooter, so look up for chipped bricks as well as down."

"Can't be too skilled. He missed."

"Thank God."

Daniel slowly scrutinized the wall, brick by brick, inch by inch, using his hands to go over the lower bricks. Jesse copied his actions.

"If we get lucky, we'll find an actual hole. Chips might indicate the bullet was deflected, but looking around here, I don't see anything that would cause deflection."

"Here," shouted Jesse after about ten minutes. "Think I found something."

Jesse pointed to a hole lodged low, hidden by the thick hedge. Daniel fished out his Swiss Army knife, slipped his left hand into a latex glove, and pulled a small plastic bag out of his pocket.

"Hey, Mr. Boy Scout. Do you always carry evidence bags and gloves with you?"

"Old habits die hard. Cops are always on duty."

Daniel took a few photos with his cell and then got down to business. Kneeling next to the wall, he stuck the point of the knife into the hole and wiggled it to free the slug. It dropped into his gloved hand.

"A little smashed, but the lab techs should be able to process it."

He held position, twisted around, and looked up.

"Go back and stand where you were standing."

Jesse complied. "What are you thinking?"

"To get this angle, the shooter had to be up high. He could have been up there." Daniel pointed to the parking garage about a block away.

"About two hundred yards, give or take. High-powered rifle. Definitely with a scope."

"Professional?"

"Would be my guess. Piss anybody off lately?"

"I'm always pissing people off. But add it to what I told you about being followed and I'll bet it's all connected. Especially since I found a GPS tracker in my backpack."

"That solidifies the being tailed part. Let me see it."

"I've left it in the backpack so whoever it is won't know he's been made."

"Smart."

"When we get back to your house I'll show it to you."

Daniel sighted the probable bullet flight path again. "Curious why he missed." He stood up and brushed off the knees of his jeans. "Maybe he missed on purpose. Just trying to scare you, like Morgan's phone calls."

"It takes more than being shot at to scare me. Just makes me work harder, because I know if someone's trying to scare me off or kill me then I'm on the right track."

"But to what end?"

"Ah, the million-dollar question. What is someone afraid I'll find out?"

"Good question."

Howie awoke and stared, bleary-eyed, at the ceiling fan whirling overhead. The sun was shining into the room.

Momentarily disoriented, he rubbed his eyes, trying to remember where he was. It wasn't his mom's house. He was alone in the bed, but could see a long red hair curled on the pillow beside him. *Is someone else here?* His eyes shot to the bathroom, but the door was open. *Was I with someone last night?*

He groped for the remote and turned on the TV. When he heard the announcer talking about the stock market's phenomenal rise, he realized it was Monday, not Sunday. He'd blown away a full day. Sunday was lost. He fell back against the pillows. *Howie the screwup strikes again.* Thank God he listened to Moss and paid for a month's rental on the storage unit, since he hadn't cleared out the stuff in the required twenty-four hours.

"Enough! Get your ass out of bed, boy. It's your big day. Time to make magic."

Maybe a day later than planned, but today was going to be great. He could feel the excitement down to his toes. Bob Smith had told him he could have everything left in the storage unit.

He planned to assess each item's potential sale price and take photos for eBay. He rubbed his hands together. The items that weren't his to sell should definitely be gone by now.

His mouth felt like an army had tramped through it. Sitting up, looking out the window, he could see the familiar orange and pink Dunkin' Donuts sign. His stomach growled. He rubbed his face, then pulled the sheet away, got up, twisted the blinds to shut out some light, and went to the bathroom to pee. His pounding head told him he'd tied one on. And the soreness between his legs and the love bite he saw on his neck when he looked in the mirror left little doubt that he hadn't spent the night alone.

Howie flushed the toilet and stumbled out of the bathroom, cursed when he caught his toe on a chair leg, but turned white when he saw Moss sitting on the edge of the bed.

"How the fuck did you get in here?"

"Does it matter? I'm here."

"What the hell do you want?"

"Get dressed." Howie caught the boxers Moss flung in his direction.

His hands shook slightly, and he wobbled as he shoved his right leg and then his left into his shorts.

"Funny," laughed Moss, "I pegged you for a briefs man."

Howie eyed his backpack sitting on the credenza where he kept a Ruger LCP tucked in the front pocket, loaded and ready.

"Go for it." Moss chuckled. "If you think you can make it. I dare you." Their eyes met. "Of course, these might be helpful." Moss hurled a handful of bullets at him.

Howie ripped open the backpack and checked the gun. He could tell it was empty by its weight. He turned away from Moss, scratching and adjusting his privates, his penis sore and inflamed. Had he caught a case of crabs from whichever broad he'd been with?

"What the fuck do you want?"

Their eyes locked. He who blinked first lost, and Howie was determined it wouldn't be him.

"I've got one question to start our day's festivities." Moss leveled his gaze at Howie. "Who are you working for?"

"No one."

"Please. I know better. You didn't just buy unit seventy-five on a whim. You were hired to buy it. And after you did, you locked it faster than a crowd of shoppers racing for sales on black Friday. Didn't make any sense to me, so I paid a little midnight call on the storage facility. Imagine my surprise when a van pulled up and two men loaded almost all the cartons from the unit into it."

"Did they leave the bike?"

"You dumb little shit. Do you have any idea what was in those cartons?"

"No." He ran his fingers through his hair and dry-rubbed his face. *God, I need a fix.*

"I'll give you three guesses, and the first two don't count."

"Who gives a shit what was in the boxes? You said the bike and that wooden screen were worth lots of money, so if all they took were boxes what do I care?" Howie gritted his teeth. "It's too early for the third degree. Get out and let me get dressed. I've got stuff to do."

"Fortunately, I care. I saw a blacked-out Merck label on one of the boxes. So the answer to my question is drugs. I'm guessing opioids, which can do a lot of damage. You're working for people who are supplying drugs. How does that make you feel, shithead?"

Howie crumpled like a cheap suit, falling into the chair that moments before had smashed his toe.

"I didn't know. Ya gotta believe me."

"I don't gotta believe you, but you are going to make it right."

"How?"

"You're working for me now, kid. And I'm not a benevolent boss."

"Wait. I don't think I can do this. I don't want to do this."

Moss got up close and personal in Howie's face, nostrils flaring, eyes ablaze, fists balled, his temper on the brink of exploding. "I don't give a shit what you want or don't want." His words were low, slow, and seething. "You need to understand who you're dealing with on all sides of this operation. These are people you don't want to mess with."

"But…"

"There's no 'but.' Only yes, sir. Thank you, sir."

"But I…"

"You're in too deep to find religion now. Should have thought of that before you took their money. Now your only calculation is how badly do you want to see tomorrow?" Moss leaned in, a hair's breadth away from Howie's nose. "Get dressed. And take a shower, for God's sake. You stink."

Howie turned away from Moss and headed for the bathroom.

"I'll be right outside the door."

Twenty minutes later the door to the room opened and a freshly shaven and showered Howie stood at the railing next to Moss. His raked his fingers through his wet hair, then he gripped the second floor railing like it was his last lifeline to salvation.

"This isn't what I planned. The drugs, I mean. How was I to know?"

"Life is full of disappointments, kid. Get over it. Let's go."

CHAPTER 15

"Are you sure he can't see me?"

"Yes, Mrs. Lee," said Detective Knight. "This is one-way glass. On the other side it looks like a mirror. He's probably seen lineups on TV shows, so he knows someone is back here, but he won't be able to see you."

"I'm really nervous."

"Don't worry," said the woman who entered the room. "You'll do fine. I'm Wendy Holland, the district attorney for James City County, Mrs. Lee. It's nice to meet you."

There was a knock at the door and a man wearing a suit came in. "Colin Faraday, representing the defense." He handed Knight a business card. "Thanks for waiting for me."

"Now that we're all here, let's get started." Knight reached up for the curtain cord. "You'll see six men when I open the curtains. All you have to do is look at them and tell me if you see the man who sold you the insulin at the flea market. Then you'll be escorted out and we'll do the rest."

Mrs. Lee took a deep breath. "I've seen this a million times on *Law and Order,* but bless my heart, I never thought I'd be doing it myself."

"You'll do fine." Knight touched her arm. "Are you ready?"

"Yes. I suppose so."

Mrs. Lee gasped as the curtains parted and six men shuffled in. Each one held a numbered card to his chest.

"Number one step forward." Knight continued down the line, asking each man to step forward and then return to his spot.

"Well, does anyone look like the man who sold you the insulin?" asked the district attorney.

"They all kinda look alike, don't they?"

"We're not trying to trick you, Mrs. Lee," said Knight. "Just take your time."

"Number four. I think it was him."

"But you're not sure?" asked Faraday.

Mrs. Lee turned her head and glared at Faraday. "I'm sure. Very sure. He's the man who sold me the insulin that hurt my Lette."

Knight spoke into the intercom. "We're done. Thank you." He turned to Mrs. Lee. "Thank you."

"Did I do okay? I know it was him, number four."

"I'm afraid we can't say any more at this point. I'll have one of my officers take you home."

"Interested in more work?" asked Bob Smith when Howie answered his cell.

"Sure. What do you have in mind?"

"Not over the phone. Meet me at Longhorn again. Two o'clock today, and I'll give you the details."

They ordered beers and appetizers.

"You seem a little nervous, Howie. I can feel your leg bouncing under the table. Everything okay?"

"Yeah. I'm just excited about all the stuff in the shed that I can sell. Did you know there was an antique motorcycle in there?"

"Nope. Didn't know that." Bob smiled. "Glad to see you're profiting from our little venture. I love riding. What type was it?"

"Indian Chief. An old one. I've sold it already or I'd let you make me an offer."

"Aren't you the little entrepreneur?" Bob sipped his beer and ate one of the corn fritters. "I love these things. So much better than hushpuppies." He ate another one.

"So what's this next job you want to talk about?" Howie's nerves were on edge. Moss had him wired for sound and was listening to every word of their conversation.

"This is a transportation job, nothing more. You'll pick up a truck and drive it to Lenexa."

"Where the hell is Lenexa?"

"Not even a half an hour north of Williamsburg. Just up Route 60."

"What's the payload?"

"Nothing you need to concern yourself with."

Howie shifted in his seat. "Are you talking something illegal? I think I have a right to know what I'm transporting."

"Just some of the stuff my associates removed from the storage shed. A few cartons."

"Okay." Howie blew out a breath. "That seems easy enough."

"And you can keep the rest of the money that was in the envelope."

"Thanks."

"Consider it a bonus for a job well done. So far you've made a nice little profit from our venture. Paying a thousand for the shed left you with four thousand dollars by my calculation."

"Thanks."

"It goes without saying that you can't make a traditional bank deposit with any of this cash," said Bob. "Put it someplace safe, just not a bank…unless it's a safety deposit box."

"I don't have one of those."

"Stick it under your mattress for all I care. Get what I'm saying?"

"Yeah, Bob. Don't worry."

Without a word, Bob took a photo of Howie with his cellphone.

"What's that for?"

"The guy you're picking up wants to know what you look like."

"Who's the guy I'm picking up?"

"Security."

"Then it's a good thing he's riding shotgun," laughed Howie. "Do you have a picture of him so I know I'm picking up the right guy?"

"You'll know. Don't worry. There won't be any doubt."

"When am I leaving? I've gotta tell my mom I'm shoving off, and it'll look funny if I just disappear without letting her know."

"Not a problem. It won't be for a few days. Like last time, I'll call you."

Soraya walked into The Hay-Adams, her favorite hotel in DC precisely at 12:45 and posed at the entrance to the Lafayette restaurant, her bejeweled hand resting on her hip. She swept the elegant room for her luncheon companion, relishing all the adoring eyes turned in her direction, imagining how many of the men would find it difficult to stand, let alone walk, right now.

"Right this way, ma'am," said the maître d'. He held her chair and placed two menus on the table. "Senator Whitley called to say he would be a few minutes late."

"Thank you. A glass of Veuve Clicquot La Grande Dame, please."

The table was in a secluded corner with a view of Lafayette Square and the White House, but Soraya chose the seat that faced the open room, her back to the windows.

"I'm sorry to have kept you waiting Soraya," said Senator Whitley, his lips brushing her cheek. "A congressman's work is never-ending. The view is so lovely here. Don't you agree?"

Her champagne and his drink arrived together.

"I see you're a regular. Do they already know what you're having for lunch?" Soraya gazed at Whitley over the rim of her champagne glass as he settled himself in his seat and put his napkin on his lap. *Common interests make strange bedfellows.*

"Perhaps I dine here a bit too often, but one can't beat the ambiance. And DC is a see and be seen world."

The waiter approached and took their order.

"Shall we enjoy lunch before business?" asked Whitley.

"There's not much to discuss. Things are moving along. We had a minor setback, but the first shipment left on time."

"Yes. I know. And the rest?"

"Will be delivered promptly. I might suggest closing the Williamsburg hub, relocating to someplace less popular."

Whitley's phone rang. "Excuse me." He listened, saying little.

Soraya watched for telltale gestures, but he was a tough man to read. Like many good politicians, his face was a blank canvas. He ended the call and faced her.

"It seems you've already taken steps to move our operation."

"Efficiency. I thought it best." Soraya wondered who on her team was brazen enough to betray her and call Whitley directly. Whoever it was would pay a hefty price for his actions.

"And when were you planning to tell me?"

"I'm telling you now."

"May I know where?"

"Do you think that's wise? If anything goes wrong, plausible deniability would serve you better than a slip of the tongue in the heat of a gaggle of reporters throwing questions at you."

"Soraya, I've been at this game a long time. In fact, I've been thinking about retiring, especially if our business becomes as lucrative as you've led me to believe it can."

Soraya sipped her champagne and stared across the room at all the power players enjoying their lunch.

"Who might take your place? Your committee assignment wields a great deal of power."

"And I've enjoyed every minute of it, but it's time. I've been grooming my chief of staff to slip into my shoes, giving her more and more visibility so the people of Pennsylvania know who she is when I announce my plans." He buttered a piece of roll. "So where did you move our goods?"

"If you must. A campground in Lenexa. Funny as it sounds, there's a good little Italian restaurant there. That's how I found the place. And it has direct access to the Chickahominy River."

"All the comforts of home." Whitley finished his drink and nodded to the waiter for another. "And when will this move take place?"

"In the next few days. I've got the driver and security in place. Just need to rent the truck."

Whitley's phone rang again. He looked at the caller ID, rose from the table just as lunch arrived. "Enjoy your lunch. An emergency I must attend to has come to my attention. I must be going. Let me know when everything is finalized."

CHAPTER 16

Jesse wandered around the Historic District, his mind swirling with all the information Ravi shared about what had been in the vials. If he could just make the connections that were eluding him, he knew he and Morgan could write a bang-up, tell-all story. Hopefully this aimless wandering would propel his brain into hyper mode and things would fall into place.

He needed to talk to Morgan—

He'd been calling her all day. Where the hell was she?

Suddenly fear for Morgan's safety overwhelmed him. He'd checked his phone repeatedly, but no messages came through from her or about her. Two empty vials sat in the front pocket of his backpack.

His cell finally rang, displaying her number.

"Morgan? Where the hell have you been."

"No. *Je suis désolé*. It is not your beloved one. But it could be…soon…if you cooperate."

"Who is this?"

"I think you know the answer to that. We have business to conduct. Are you ready?"

Morgan opened her eyes. Her head throbbed, but with her hands tied behind her back she couldn't feel what she was sure was an egg-size bump on her forehead.

Where am I?

She blinked several times, letting her eyes adjust to the dim light of the space contrasted with the sun's glare framing three sides of the door. She was lying on a hard cement floor in a small space, maybe twenty by twenty. Cold. So icy cold she was actually shivering. She could see her exhales, wisps of breath momentarily captured in the slim light penetrating the darkness of her prison.

What's that smell?

Gasoline?

A garage? I'm on the floor of a friggin' garage.

And it's light outside.

"Focus, girl. Don't panic."

Throbbing pain and a foggy brain clouded her thinking. Moving slowly, Morgan assessed her predicament. Her hands and feet were bound, but nothing hurt except the dull ache in her head. She still had her clothes on and her shoes.

"Hello? Anybody here?"

Silence. The feeling of being alone, with no one knowing where she was, overwhelmed her.

Alone works. No one can hurt me if there's no one else here.

She checked the bindings. Duct tape. She remembered watching a YouTube video about escaping from duct tape. *If I can get untied...if I can get the door open...I can run, find a phone, and call Jesse. Two big ifs—better than the alternative of waiting around here.*

It all happened so fast. What's the last thing I remember?

A cryptic text from Jesse to meet at Peking for lunch. Her brief moment of eye contact with the driver of the car who quickly pulled next to her, so close to her car that she had to twist sideways to get out. She was about to curse at him about how close his car was to hers when her stomach clutched and she sensed danger. Too late when she realized the car that pulled into the parking space next to her was a black SUV. Too late when her gut clenched. Too late when her eyes met those of the driver, his cold, incisive, razor-sharp stare slicing through her.

Powerful arms had me in a bear hug. All I could do was kick. But my kicks didn't land on anything solid, only air, as I struggled and squirmed and tried to break his hold. I tried to turn to see who was attacking me. Then a weird snapping sound. Burning on my back. My head started to spin. I felt myself falling, losing control.

A door opened. Light spilled into the space. Footsteps. A tall, well-dressed man approached her and stopped less than a foot away. He smiled down at her, untwisting the cap from a bottle of water.

"What do you want with me?"

"We'll get to that. First things first. Are you thirsty? Would you like some water?" He proffered the bottle, touching it to her lips.

Morgan clenched her lips tightly closed and turned her head away. He pulled back the bottle of water.

"Suit yourself." He recapped the bottle and placed it on the floor beside her.

"Who are you? Do you know who I am?"

"Yes. Of course I know who you are. I don't make a habit of grabbing strangers off the street."

"What do you want? I'm not afraid of you."

"Maybe not now. But you will be soon."

But Morgan was too busy calculating the dangers of her current predicament and the odds of escape to respond to his threat.

"Are you going to kill me?"

"Not unless your boyfriend, Mr. Sinclair, forces our hand."

"What's that supposed to mean?"

"He and we are negotiating."

"Over me? Over my life?" White-hot fear pulsed through her, but she fought to maintain her composure.

"You are an innocent bystander here. A pawn. It is unfortunate for your sake." She flinched when he touched her cheek.

They can't kill me...can they? Of course not. This is America.

Images of horrific stories zoomed through her mind like a news reel on speed. Shit. Her courage evaporated faster than water on hot cement. *People disappear and get killed every day.* She wrote about their misery, chronicled their stories.

Fighting to restrain her fear, sensing her captor would laugh should she lash out at him, Morgan struggled to calm her thoughts. She needed a better strategy if she was going to save herself. Her reporter training kicked in. Who, what, when, where, why, and how. She knew who the players were, the where and when were fairly obvious.

"What do you want? What's the negotiation?"

"Ah, you want details." His smirk unnerved her. "But, yes, you are a reporter, are you not?"

"It's my life we're talking about. Don't you think I have a right to know the stakes?"

"American women." He shook his head. "I will never understand why you want to be equal to men, when you were created to be far superior. Men put you on a pedestal to adore you, but you American women, you could not jump off fast enough."

"How patronizing. Your pedestal is a rape culture, one that condones female circumcision, treating women as property, and making us slaves."

"That is not me, nor my countrymen. If this ends well for you, and I pray for your sake that it does, you must come visit France, see its beauty, feel its love."

"France?"

"Yes, my sweet, France."

"But I thought…I assumed…"

"That because I have dark skin, and speak with an accent, and because of Mr. Sinclair's recent visit to Africa, that I am African."

Morgan opened her mouth but no words came out. Her mind reeled.

"No comeback?" He raised an eyebrow. "I have enjoyed our little chat, but I am afraid I must leave you now. Someone will be along shortly to see to your comfort."

"Good. I have to pee."

"All in good time. All in good time. We will speak again soon, and I will hopefully have good news for you. Until then, *adieu.*"

The slamming door broadcast finality, and Morgan couldn't tear her eyes away from it and the thin slice of light. *What if he doesn't come back? Gets hit by a car and killed? Or worse? Who else knows I'm here? What if no one ever finds me? I could starve to death all alone, and no one would know. People would miss me. Jesse. Rachel. My parents. Coworkers. They'll wonder what happened to me.*

She shuddered as her tears fell like rain.

"I like when we work together, Moss," said Daniel. "Pool our resources and lay everything out. None of the red tape and formal, compartmentalized bullshit the alphabets are forced to deal with."

"They have their orders, and bureaucrats are nothing if not good at following orders. I'm surprised you've lasted as long as you have in your contract FBI gig."

"You and me both." Daniel poured two cups of coffee. "So what have we got?"

"Got what?" asked Rachel as she walked into the kitchen, her arms loaded with groceries.

Daniel and Moss exchanged glances. "Have you seen Morgan today?" Daniel asked, as nonchalantly as he could.

"Yeah." Rachel slid the bags onto the counter. "She brought over a new teddy bear for little Madeline next door." Looking first at Daniel and then at Moss, her brow crinkled. "What's happened?"

"Jesse is on his way. Let's wait until he gets here."

It didn't take long to hear the squeal of tires, a car door slam, and see Jesse barrel into the kitchen.

"What gives?" asked Daniel.

"Listen." Jesse put his phone on the table between them and hit the play button.

"I have something of yours. And you have something that belongs to me. I suggest a trade."

"Who is this? Is Morgan okay? If you've hurt her—"

"Please, Mr. Sinclair. We are not barbarians. This is business. A simple exchange, then we all go our merry way."

"Let me talk to Morgan." Jesse mouthed the words "French accent" to the group.

"Impossible. I am afraid at the moment that is not possible, but I understand your desire for, what do you call it, *preuve de vie*, proof of life."

"Make it happen or no deal." Jesse disconnected, not waiting for a reply. He knew the guy would call back. There was too much at stake for him not to. Whoever he was, he had too much to lose. So did Morgan.

Jesse clicked off the recording and pinched the bridge of his nose, fighting back tears, before making eye contact with everyone.

"He used Morgan's phone."

"Slick app for recording calls. When did the call come in?" asked Moss.

Jesse looked at the time stamp. "Two fifteen."

"When was the last time you actually spoke to her?"

"Early this morning, before my meeting," said Jesse.

"That normal?" asked Daniel, pocketing his cell phone and pouring a cup of coffee for Jesse.

"Some days."

"But she was meeting you for lunch." said Rachel, her fear for her friend evident to everyone.

"No she wasn't."

"Yes, she was. She was here and got a text from you to meet at Peking. She was surprised because she wasn't expecting you until dinnertime."

"What time was she here?" asked Daniel.

Rachel eyed the three men cautiously. "Around eleven thirty. We were going to play some mahj, but then she got a text from you inviting her to lunch so she bailed on me." Rachel glanced at the wall clock, but looked back in time to catch the glance Jesse exchanged with Daniel. "She said she'd be back by three to play."

"But you didn't text her?" Daniel looked at Jesse.

"I've been in a meeting with a possible publisher for the big pharma story. Then I took a walk around the colonial area to clear my head and try to get all these pieces to fit together. When we talked this morning, she planned to stop at Publix to pick up a roast chicken for dinner. I told her not to bother, we'd go out, but she insisted, saying she wanted a hot bath, some wine and a quiet night at home to relax."

"I'm calling Adam Knight," Daniel said as he left the kitchen. "He needs to be here."

"I'll have an officer show her photograph at Publix and see if anyone remembers seeing her earlier." Detective Adam Knight had joined the group quickly after Daniel's call. They'd worked together last spring to stop a black market kidney trafficking ring operating in Williamsburg, and today was his day off so he came right over when Daniel called. Now his notepad was out and Jesse had just replayed the call.

"Did you catch the accent?" asked Jesse.

"Yes, French," said Knight. "Any callback?"

"Not yet."

"You took a big chance hanging up."

"I know, but I also know that I have something this guy values. Grabbing Morgan in broad daylight was a bold move. He's not going to end this until he gets what he wants."

"And what do you think that is?" asked Knight.

Jesse hesitated.

"Now is not the time to be secretive," said Rachel. "I know you're a reporter and it's baked into your brains not to share details, but Morgan's life may be at stake."

Jesse rubbed his face and looked warily at Detective Knight.

"Let's start with an easier, more comfortable question," said Knight. "Do you know what was on her schedule today?"

"Yes." He started pacing the room. "And no." He flung up his arms. "She doesn't tell me every detail of any of her days. She said she was going to the library."

"Scotland Street? Or the branch in Croaker?"

"Croaker, I think. She didn't want to be disturbed, and she always runs into people she knows at the one on Scotland Street."

"Okay. Where else?"

Jesse's mind was blank. "That's all I know. It's not like we're connected at the hip and I keep tabs on her every move. And Rachel just said she was here and they were going to play mah jongg, which was not what she told me."

"And her cell goes to voice mail?"

"Been ringing her every five minutes until I got this call. She never picked up. Either she won't because she's annoyed that I'm checking up on her..." Jesse looked directly at Knight. "Or...she can't."

"Let's not jump the gun, Jesse. I'll get a BOLO out on her car. White Camry, right?

"Yeah. It's got Gadsden plates, but I don't know the number."

"We'll look it up. Let me call this in. Be right back." Knight pulled out his cell phone and left the room for a few minutes.

Jesse poured himself a cup of coffee, held up the pot, and turned to the group.

"Anyone want a refill?"

"I'd love one," said Knight when he walked back into the room.

"Sorry. Where are my manners?" said Rachel. She took the pot of coffee from Jesse, poured Knight's refill, replaced the pot on the burner, and sliced and plated the coffee cake she made earlier.

"I should have been more vigilant, gone with her."

"Based on the small amount of time I've spent around Morgan," said Moss, who'd been pretty quiet up to now, "that would have gone over like a lead balloon, *and* gotten you banished to the couch for the foreseeable future."

Rachel gave him a hug. "As you said, Jesse, you're not connected at the hip. You have separate lives and things to do. We'll get to the bottom of this. It's going to be all right."

Jesse smirked. "Yeah. She wouldn't have liked that, but I knew something was wrong. I could have...should have done more to protect her...keep her safe."

"Beating yourself up isn't going to help," said Knight. "Recriminations make you feel like shit, and right now I need you sharp, firing on all cylinders, not wasting your energy on second-guessing yourself."

"What can we do?" asked Daniel.

"Sit tight at this point. Let me get things started from my end. We'll check Peking's parking lot for her car and any video surveillance." Knight reviewed his notes, then put away the pad. He looked at Jesse's phone still sitting on the table, and then at Daniel. "Don't mean to sound like my department can't handle things, but I remember when we worked together last spring, you had a special friend. You called him a cyber wizard?"

"Brett," laughed Moss.

"Right. Maybe give him a call and see if he can work some magic and backtrack the call from Jesse's phone. Maybe we'll get lucky and get a number, or a cell tower, or some identifying information."

"Can't your department do that?" asked Rachel.

"We can, but we have to go through channels, paperwork, warrants, official stuff. Slows things down. I think your friend may be able to cut out the bullshit. But I don't want to know the how of what he does."

"I hear you," said Daniel, smirking.

"I do, however, want to know what you find out."

"Got it."

Daniel called Brett, and after exchanging pleasantries about their Florida friends, asked for help.

"Did you get the information I sent you about Morgan's prank calls?" asked Brett.

"Yes. But things have escalated here. I need another favor. Something you are uniquely qualified to provide."

"You think so?"

"I know so."

Daniel gave Brett a broad-strokes review of the current situation.

"Think you can help?"

"Does a bear shit in the woods? Of course I can help. Give me the cell number and I'll be back in touch."

In under twenty minutes Brett called back.

"That was fast," said Daniel.

"You got lucky. The number went active a few minutes ago. I've triangulated the call to Merchants Square. Whoever made the first call is there now, on the phone."

"Thanks Brett," yelled Jesse while he grabbed his backpack and raced out of the kitchen.

"Should I be telling the gang to plan a trip to Virginia?"

"No. I think we can handle this locally."

"They'll be bummed. They love Rachel's cooking."

CHAPTER 17

It was late Thursday afternoon and the tourist crowds had thinned, so securing a patio table at the Fat Canary was no problem. Emmanuel Matamba settled himself, took the proffered menu, and ordered a glass of white wine. His gaze ran over the few families corralling tired, screaming children and panting dogs. An elegantly dressed couple walked by, perused the menu, but decided not to sit down. A pity, he thought. Fat Canary had an excellent reputation for fine cuisine and a brilliant wine selection. His phone rang.

"Emmanuel, darling. How are you enjoying your foray into America's past?"

"We need to change our plans," said Emmanuel.

"I'm afraid that's impossible."

Emmanuel nodded at the waiter, who set down the glass of wine and he pointed to the tuna tempura appetizer for his order.

"Maybe you do not understand, it is a tad hot out here, and I do not mean global warming."

"Things are already in motion. Our partners are not the type of people you disappoint. Money has changed hands. Buyers are waiting."

"The authorities are watching my movements. I expect to be invited in to answer questions very soon."

"Pull diplomatic immunity."

"That will only delay the inevitable. It will not take long for them to check my status and realize that I am not who I claim to be."

"Just be your charming self and leave your status to me. Speak French. It'll take them awhile to find a translator."

"My dear, the situation has changed," stressed Matamba. "Tests have been run at a reputable lab."

"That is most unfortunate," said the caller.

"Mr. Sinclair was less than cooperative when we initially spoke. We have had to take more robust action to get his attention."

"And has it worked?"

"Only time will tell. What's our next step?"

"I'll make the necessary calls to ensure that an appropriate diversion is initiated. We'll get the press looking over there so we can conclude our business over here."

"Brilliant, as usual. What about outside the US?"

"Product is moving smoothly in other venues."

"How do we get our local train back on its tracks?"

"We're moving the goods to a new location. A quiet little campgrounds with river access."

"You seem to have everything handled."

"Comme ci, comme ça. Au revoir."

As Emmanuel pocketed his phone, the waiter brought his food. *"Merci."*

And a stranger sat down at his table. But he wasn't a stranger. Matamba had been following him since he left the Congo.

"May I join you?"

"It appears you already have. Can I get you something, Mr...?"

Jesse flipped open his press credentials. "Nothing for me, thank you. If you don't mind, I'd like a few words."

"I prefer to eat in peace, but far be it from me to refuse to accommodate a member of the esteemed American press."

Jesse waved the waiter away after asking for a glass of water only.

"I hope you're enjoying your stay in Colonial Williamsburg."

"It is a quaint little town, rich in the history of the founding of your nation." Emmanuel deftly used chopsticks to lift a piece of tempura, dip it into wasabi and pop it into his mouth. *"Très magnifique."* He blotted his mouth with a napkin. "Are you sure you won't have something? My treat."

"No. Thank you." Jesse sipped his water. "I was wondering if I might inquire about the reason for your visit to our little town."

"You might inquire about anything you wish, but alas, I am a man with diplomatic immunity, an emissary of the Congolese government, so my responses might not be what you want to hear. In fact, your being here, and this conversation, are not in keeping with the spirit of diplomatic immunity. Am I being charged with something?"

"Have you done something illegal?"

"Not that I am aware of."

"That's good, because I have no charging authority, although I do have friends who do. We're a tad curious about your business here. It isn't often we get a visitor of your stature without a full entourage."

"And who, may I ask, is 'we?'"

"Some friends." Deciding to up the ante, Jesse added, "One of whom was shot at the other day. Another of whom has disappeared."

"And you are accusing me?"

141

"No…no…nothing like that. That same friend thinks he's being followed by a SUV with diplomatic plates. And when you combine that with you being here…in Williamsburg… by yourself…without even a bodyguard…and my friend's disappearance, it all seems a strange coincidence, don't you agree?"

"Is this an official inquiry? If so, I would like to know which news organization you represent."

Jesse twisted the glass of water in his hands, knowing he was out of bounds. "Not an official inquiry. Think of it as a friendly conversation. Like the one we shared when we first met at Dulles a few weeks ago."

"With all due respect, we are not friends. I am sitting here, having a light snack, enjoying the scenery, and I resent being accosted by you. Notwithstanding my diplomatic immunity, I have every right to be here. Yours is a free country, the envy of the world in that regard. Unless you want me to file a complaint with your State Department, I suggest you leave, and we shall pretend this encounter never happened."

Jesse stood. "By your leave, Mr. Matamba."

"You know my name."

"I know a great deal about you, the least of which is your name. I'm certain our paths will cross again, and your diplomatic immunity won't be sufficient to prevent a more robust conversation." Jesse placed the two empty vials on the table. "Enjoy your lunch."

"Twice in one day," said Soraya when she answered the phone. "We're speaking too often."

"The situation has changed again, and I thought you should know."

"Go on."

"It appears Mr. Sinclair has seen the error of his ways and has since relented and returned the vials. But they are empty. Getting them back is now moot."

"Make them disappear. Without the physical vials, a good lawyer will be able to refute any evidence produced because we would want to confirm any lab tests, which empty vials makes impossible."

"No vials to test makes the situation even better. It becomes a he said, she said."

"Precisely. And the girl? I assume she will be released unharmed."

"Consider it done." Matamba ended the call, troubled by Soraya's closing comments. How did she know a girl was involved? He had only indicated that more robust actions were taken, never mentioning what they were. But Soraya knew. And knowing that she knew unnerved him. *What else does she know?*

Jesse walked away, grateful for Brett's cyber skills. It's very reassuring to have friends in discreet places. From his command center in Florida, Brett was able to back track Jesse's first call to a cell tower just outside Colonial Williamsburg. And they'd gotten lucky because the same phone had received another call.

Jesse had raced out of Rachel's home, across Monticello, down Richmond Road and across South Henry Street, slipping into a parking spot in the garage, which put him in Merchants Square just as the call disconnected. Talk about being in the right place at the right time. Jesse saw his target, the man from the airport, assessed his approach, and went to work.

When he left Mr. Matamba, he didn't go far. From the benches in front of the Barnes and Noble bookstore, Jesse watched his target finish his lunch, make a phone call, pay his bill, and leave the Fat Canary. Matamba crossed South Henry Street and headed for the two-hour parking lot behind the ticket office. Jesse crossed slowly, keeping well back, wanting to zero in on Matamba's car so he could identify it for Detective Knight. But Matamba kept going. He walked up North Henry Street to Francis Street and made a left.

There's nothing up there. Except... The Williamsburg Inn. That's where he's going.

Jesse spun around and raced back the way he'd come, reached his car in record time, zoomed out of the garage onto Henry Street, and backtracked his route. If he was lucky and made the light at Henry and Francis Streets, he'd catch up to Matamba while he was still walking to the Inn. Unless Jesse's guess was wrong.

Target acquired. There was Matamba, not twenty feet ahead of him. Jesse slowed to a crawl, not wanting to pass the man, who had just entered the Inn's property and was heading for the main doors. It was barely four o'clock, so Jesse easily found a parking space in the small lot reserved for guests of the Kings Arms Tavern. He scribbled a note saying he was going to the tavern for a four o'clock job interview and tucked it under his windshield wiper. He grabbed his backpack from the trunk of his car and headed up the curved sidewalk after Matamba.

Enjoying the warmth of the fireplace in the Williamsburg Inn's lobby, Soraya Rousseau sat sipping Crown Royal over ice. Kidnapping was not her favorite remedy, but there were times when it was necessary. Of course in her world, death usually followed. No witnesses. She suspected Matamba was not of the same mindset and would release the girl without harm. Another loose end that would need to be tied.

She watched Matamba enter the lobby and head for the elevators.

"He looks frazzled." Her words, meant for no one's ears, confirmed her impression during her call. Then she saw Jesse come through the doors.

"Interesting. This guy's good."

She'd watched his encounter with Matamba from the steps of the Craft House, but hadn't realized he followed Matamba to the Inn. "I wonder how good."

Her approach was priceless, her feminine whiles on full display. "Excuse me. It looks like you just came from the tourist area. I was told by friends to make sure I saw whatever was playing at the Kimball theater, but I can't seem to find where the theater actually is."

Jesse's attention was abruptly pulled away from his prey, who was at the elevators, to the woman standing in front of him. And what he saw caused a twitch between his legs. Her leopard leggings showcased a lithe body and legs that wouldn't quit, while a black tunic hugged enticing breasts. Add to that long blonde hair, ice-blue eyes that flashed from a face with mere trace features defining her as mixed race.

"The Kimball?" His mind reeled. "I-I don't know. I'm sorry. I've got to go." He rushed away, leaving Soraya standing alone in the lobby.

Okay. Maybe he's not that good. Clearly he can't think on his feet. A two-bit reporter trying to undermine Matamba with his mere presence? Too funny for words.

She returned to her seat, finished her brandy, ordered another, and pulled out her phone.

"Director Obi, so nice to speak with you again."

"I wasn't expecting to hear from you so soon."

"A situation has arisen. I need your help to solidify the diplomatic credentials for a friend of mine."

Obi's response had Soraya chuckling.

"Of course, you can do this, Director. When I hang up, you'll make a phone call, get my friend's name added to the Congolese delegation from WHO, and thank the person graciously."

Soraya sipped her drink, holding the phone away from her ear while Obi listed her objections.

"Then it's settled. The name is Emmanuel Matamba. See that it's done within the hour."

A second call was made to Renata with instructions to call once she could confirm completion of the orders just given to Obi. Taking another sip of brandy, Soraya made a mental list of the people who would have to disappear once this operation was over. It was growing longer every day.

How many people can I make disappear without creating problems for myself?

She knew who she wanted to do the job—Moss, a man as ruthless as she. If only she could convince him to assist her and then leave with her. There were places in the South Pacific where they could live like royalty, having the funds to enjoy the best life could buy.

She gave the server a fifty with instructions to forget her entirely should someone come asking questions. No one was going to prevent her from completing this mission. There was too much money at stake. And it was hers. All hers. If people died, so be it. Not her concern.

CHAPTER 18

Morgan took a deep breath and stared at the stars. The last thing she remembered was the nauseating, sickly-sweet smell that permeated the garage and invaded her senses.

And now seeing stars told her that night had fallen and she was outdoors. She was free.

They let me go?

A full moon shone like a spotlight in the sky. She was prone in a field, free of all restraints. Her skin felt clammy, and she swatted at crawly things tickling her legs and arms. She checked her Apple watch, which was now back on her wrist. Just past midnight. But the day scared her. The watch face showed Thursday, but she'd gone to meet Jesse at Peking for lunch on Tuesday. A whole day. She'd lost an entire day.

A quick body scan told her she was unhurt physically. She sat up. Movement caught her eye to the left. A deer peered at her through the brush, ears twitching before it scampered away, followed by two fawns. Morgan smiled. Surely it was a sign from God.

When she tried to stand, her head spun. Steadying herself, she took a few tentative steps and turned around slowly to get her bearings. Trees. Lots of trees. No buildings. No lights.

In the distance she saw a lone car drive by. None followed behind it, which told her she was not near a main road.

"Colonial Parkway. I'm on Colonial Parkway," she whispered.

In the distance she could see glimpses of the river dancing in the moonlight.

"Rachel and Daniel live near the river. Maybe I can find their house."

Wiping beads of sweat off her forehead, she headed for the river bank.

Ahhhgh!

Morgan lost her footing and slid down the embankment on her butt, landing inches shy of the water. Stunned, she hugged her knees to her chest to keep her mud-caked sandals out of the water. She wasn't hurt so much as damp, muddy, and exhausted. She sat up. Tears trickled down her cheeks.

"No, damn it. I'm not going to cry," she declared, louder this time. "I'm free. I've got to make it to Rachel's."

Morgan boosted herself to her feet, smoothed her muddy shirt, brushed off some of the caked mud, then slowly, her strappy sandals sinking deep into mud, she made her way back to solid ground. Deciding to stay off the roadway, she moved through the trees, keeping the river on her left and the road in the distance on her right, clinging to the darkness for cover.

Dawn began to make its presence known behind her in the eastern sky. Morgan's calves burned, her breaths mere gasps as she tramped through the woods flanking the south side of Colonial Parkway while tree branches whipped her face and roots clawed at her ankles. Panting, Morgan knew she was headed in the right direction when she saw signs for the turnoff at Jamestown Settlement.

"It's Jamestown, for God's sake. There's got to be security. It's a friggin' National Park. Someone's got to be there."

Morgan gathered all her strength, left the cover of the trees, and hurried as fast as she could up to the road. No car had passed for hours. She weaved her way through the picnic tables and up to the front doors. And started banging. Banging…banging…banging.

"I kept banging and banging," she blubbered, tears flowing freely. "Someone had to be there. And there was. I was never so happy to see a uniform in my life. I grabbed him and wouldn't let go."

"Shhh." Rachel stroked Morgan's hair. "You're safe now." She bit back tears. "How do you feel?"

"Sore. Tired. Dizzy. My heart's pounding." Morgan looked at the IV in her arm and then glanced around the hospital room. "Is there any way I can get a quart or two of Gatorade? I'm starving."

"I'll never understand how you can drink that stuff."

"It's tasty. Not too sweet. Add some vodka or rum and I'm good to go. I'm hungry. Think you can find me some crackers?"

Daniel and Detective Knight had been huddled by the door. "We're on it. Be right back."

"Rachel, what did they want? Why me?"

"Later." She held her fingers to her lips, having learned from Daniel that private conversations should never be held in public spaces where unintended listeners might overhear.

"Where's Jesse?"

"He said he had an errand to run."

Morgan flopped back on the pillow. "That doesn't make sense. What kind of errand?"

"He didn't say. Just that he would get here as soon as he can. I told him I was taking you to my house, so if he misses you here, he'll know where to go."

"What kind of errand could be so important?"

"Don't trouble yourself with that right now. Let's get you cleaned up as best we can here. When they discharge you, we're going to my house for a nice hot shower and some clean clothes."

Morgan looked at her clothes piled on the chair.

"Don't think that outfit is ever going to see the light of day again. I can clean the jeans, but the silk blouse is a total loss. And those are my favorite Michael Kors sandals. They were a hundred and fifty dollars."

"Trash bin," said Rachel, trying to add a note of levity.

"On the bright side," said Morgan, "Premium Outlets is right around the corner and fall sales are on. We can go shopping."

"You bet we can. Lunch at Giuseppe's and shopping. My treat."

"I'll drink to that. Think they have any wine in here? You know, for medicinal purposes?"

"Probably not. Dr. McKenna isn't on duty this morning, but the doctor who is wants to give you a once-over before he discharges you. My steam shower is going to feel great."

Morgan grabbed Rachel's hand. "Thank you for coming."

"That's what friends are for. ER visits at six in the morning."

"Morgan was grabbed off the street in broad daylight, held incommunicado for more than a day, and then she's magically released? What's wrong with this picture?" demanded Moss. "Why did they let her go?"

"Doesn't matter how she got out," said Daniel. "Only that she did. And made it to safety."

Moss's mind was moving at light speed. "She didn't get out. They let her go. There's a difference."

"Is she okay? What did the doctors say?" Jesse raced into Rachel's kitchen, his arms loaded with a huge bouquet of red roses.

"Scraped knees, shaken up, scared, but not physically harmed. Emotional issues will definitely show up," said Daniel. "Doctor found two burn marks on her upper back. I'm assuming someone hit her with a stun gun."

"Not sure what to make of it," said Moss. "Something changed for whoever had her. But what?"

"Definitely a warning," said Daniel. "Whoever they are, they want you to know they can get to you, or someone you love. Someone wants you to back off."

"Tells me you're pissing somebody important off in a big way," said Moss.

"It's over. I gave them what they wanted," said Jesse. "I know it has to do with my Congo trip because the guy on the phone's accent was French. And they speak a lot of French in the Congo. That and the vials I took were labeled in French."

"Which you said are now empty," said Daniel.

"Right," said Jesse. "Which is why I could give them back."

"And they released Morgan after that," said Moss.

"I guess being empty didn't matter to them as long as they got the vials themselves back," said Daniel.

"Ravi's lab tests gave us the proof we needed," said Jesse. "One vial had diluted Ciprofloxacin. That and the tape of the argument I overhead between the nurse and doctor proves they knew the drugs they were using were ineffective."

"Makes you wonder about the other drugs they have." Rachel poured more coffee for everyone. "There was something on the news the other day about Ebola and the Congo. That the drugs being used weren't working and thousands of people were dying."

"Jesse, you're in someone's crosshairs," said Daniel. "You might want to reconsider what you're working on. Going full tilt could cost you or someone you care about more than your story is worth."

"But if I'm right—if the Congo and other nations are getting inferior drugs and people are dying—then that story needs to be told. We have to do something. Get to the bottom of who's approving this massacre. Because that's what it is. A massacre. Genocide. Another Holocaust."

Dead silence filled the room.

"Where is she?"

"Resting in the guest room. Down the hall. Take this." Rachel handed him a small glass of brandy.

Jesse knocked softly.

"Come in." Morgan's face ignited with a smile. She patted the side of the bed when he stopped at the doorway. "Come sit."

"How are you feeling?"

"Sore. But better now I'm here." She took a deep breath, exhaling slowly. "And safe. Roses…you got me roses."

"I'm so sorry I got you into this."

"You didn't get me into anything. We're a team, you and me, at least for our writing. What we're doing, this story… It's important. Lives may very well depend on us uncovering the truth, getting to the bottom of whatever's going on. We may not be able to stop it, but sunlight is the best defense against evil. And what these people are doing is the ultimate evil."

"I'm so glad you're safe." Jesse put the roses and the brandy on the nightstand, leaned into the bed and scooped Morgan into his arms, afraid if he let her go, she'd disappear.

"It…it was… I've never felt so powerless."

Morgan's whole body was trembling.

"Here," said Jesse, handing her the glass of brandy. "Drink this. It'll help calm you."

She clutched the glass with shaking hands, sloshing some of the amber liquid on her hand.

"I'm okay. You don't have to worry about me."

"Too late. I'm hooked." Jesse looked anywhere and everywhere but at her. "I never let myself get attached to another person. It was safer for me."

"How so?"

"The ultimate freedom. I could come and go as I pleased, sleep until two, eat ice cream for breakfast, go commando, and wear different-colored socks, and no one got in my face about it. Until now."

"And now?"

"You make a stink when I don't put the damn toilet seat cover down...and I love it. I love the way you challenge me and make my writing better than I ever could, the sexy rasp of your voice, the smile in your eyes."

Morgan smiled at him and wrapped her arms around his neck, pulling him close for a kiss.

"I hear voices. Who's here?"

"Detective Knight just showed up."

"I guess I should go talk to them."

"Only if you feel up to it."

"I'm fine." She pushed back the blanket and got up. Pulling on sweats and slipping her feet into the flip-flops Rachel brought from her house, Morgan scooped up her roses and followed Jesse to the kitchen.

"Hey, everyone," she said, welcoming their warm embraces.

"Can I refill that for you?" asked Daniel, pointing to the empty brandy glass.

"That'd be great. Thanks."

"Give me those. I'll put them in water," said Rachel.

"This may not be the best time to do this," said Knight, "but while details are fresh in your mind, could we go over what happened?"

"Sure." Morgan sipped the brandy.

"Tell us what you remember."

"I pulled into the parking lot at Peking. No one was around. That strip mall is deserted now that Kmart is closed. An SUV pulled in close, boxing me in. I was cursing a blue streak about all the empty spaces in the lot. Was about to give the driver a piece of my mind. I squeezed out and then I felt a jolt. Someone grabbed me from behind and pushed me into the SUV. And I don't remember much until I woke up on the concrete floor of a garage."

"What did he sound like? Anything unique about his voice?

"There were two of them. The first guy was tall, black, well-spoken."

"You saw his face?"

"Yeah."

"I'll get a sketch artist to come over," said Knight.

"Don't bother. I'm sure it was Matamba," said Jesse.

"Spoke with an accent. French. Told me I should make sure to visit France one day."

Jesse scrolled through the photos on his phone. This him?"

"Yes."

"What about the other guy?" asked Daniel.

"I never saw his face because he wore a mask. One of those black knit stocking things with the eyeholes."

"And you're sure it wasn't the same guy?"

"The French guy smelled different. Used an expensive cologne. Polo, I think. Something familiar. The other guy brought me water and some beef jerky. He reeked of cigarettes. Not a smell you can cover up, no matter how much cologne you use or how many showers you take."

CHAPTER 19

Rachel threw dinner together, beef stew over mashed potatoes with green beans, so the guys could talk and hash out their next steps. Now that Morgan was safe, they could make plans.

"The lab evidence is irrefutable," said Jesse. "What Marcel was given was a very diluted version of ciprofloxacin. Chicken soup would have been more beneficial. The special drug," Jesse added air quotes for effect, "was full-strength ciprofloxacin, the real juice. But by the time the doctor added it to Marcel's IV, it was already too late."

Daniel passed the bowl of mashed potatoes to Moss. "I just want to say out loud that I don't like that look in your eyes."

"What look?" asked Moss.

"That look. The one where I can almost see your wheels turning. The one that lets me know you're about to pull me out of my placid, watching-paint-dry retirement life."

"Ah, that look."

Morgan closed her eyes, willing her mind to clear. She felt like a thousand pounds of rocks were piled on her shoulders. And here was another decision, another rock, weighing her down. The men sitting around this table were ready to go to war, fight the good fight against the people who grabbed her. She wanted to scream *no, don't go,* but remained silent. She needed to think rationally, but the thoughts bombarding her consciousness were preventing her from doing so.

"You've heard of the 'perfect storm'?" said Jesse. "What we've got here is the perfect crime. Poorly made or contaminated medicines entering a third world country, sold to unsuspecting people who need them to stay alive."

"Can I add that it isn't just third world countries?" said Morgan. "Some of these tainted meds are right here in America."

"And because the fraud is hard to detect," said Jesse "big pharma is protected. The patient's continuing illness is chalked up to a serious drug reaction, or the illness getting worse, and unless and until there are numerous cases reported about a specific medication, like there was in 2008 with heparin, the faulty drug remains undetectable. It's rare to blame the drug, and because of the long supply chain, it's hard to find the source of problem. If a patient dies, it's the disease and not the ineffective drug that's listed as the cause of death. In fact, the tainted drug may never be considered or its efficacy tested. And the patient has died, so any evidence gets buried with him. And you can't go around exhuming dead people to run toxicology. It's not kosher."

"What about enforcement at the border where the medications enter the country?" asked Rachel.

"Interagency communication isn't what it should be in our country," said Daniel. "DOJ has investigators, as do ATF, the FDA, DEA, Homeland, and none of them like to play nice and share, let alone talk to the locals."

"It's not nice when the alphabets squabble," said Moss.

"So true. But squabble they must. One giant,

testosterone-laden, pissing contest." Jesse forked the last bite of beef and potatoes off his plate. "And it's worse in the destitute corners of the third world."

Detective Knight had been quietly listening to the conversation. "Mind if I add another wrinkle to the mix?"

"Be my guest," said Daniel, "but pass the potatoes first."

"I've been calling a few friends with connections."

"Is that like friends with benefits?" asked Morgan.

"Not quite," said Knight. "I'm talking military friends. And my conversations have been scary interesting. What if the Chinese decided to weaponize the drugs they manufacture?"

Jesse dropped his fork. "You're kidding, right?"

"In that scenario." Moss spread his arms wide. "We have a serious problem."

"More serious than people taking tainted meds assuming they're the real thing?" asked Rachel.

"Way more serious," said Knight. "The Chinese think long term. Always have. They play the long game, unlike American companies, who focus more on the next quarter and short-term profits. What if the Chinese saw a way to crush the US, and no one would be the wiser for years to come? They're communists after all. Their end goal is to destroy American capitalism."

"Knight, you have a sick little mind." Daniel smiled at him. "I knew there's a reason we get along."

"Thank you. But I'm not kidding. Debra has been filling my head with all sorts of information about the alerts she gets about drug interactions and efficacy."

"Pillow talk certainly has changed," laughed Rachel.

"Over eighty percent of the active ingredients in our pharmaceuticals come from China. They're shipped to other places, excipients are added to manufacture the pill, capsule, injectable, or patch, and then the finished med is shipped to a wholesaler or distributor, who gets it to the pharmacy or hospital."

"That matches my research," said Morgan. "And in my never to be humble opinion, it leaves us way too exposed."

"Take it one step further. Understanding China's desire to surpass America as the preeminent global superpower, and based on what you two have already told us about where most active ingredients come from—"

"China."

"Exactly," said Knight. "We already know the Chinese do extensive biological warfare research, but what if the Chinese decided to weaponize the pharmaceutical supply they export to us? Our military could be devastated."

"Take it one step further," said Moss. "What if the Chinese seeded a particular medication used a lot by the military—say an antibiotic—with a hallucinogenic agent that they could control?"

"Now you're talking crazy," said Morgan.

"Am I? *Manchurian Candidate* ring any bells?"

"It was a movie—two movies actually—but I see where you're going and I don't like it," said Jesse. "Plus, my friend Ravi hinted at the very same scenario. Called it 'Made in China 2025.'"

"I've heard of that program. And none of this is for you to like," said Moss. "Tampering can occur at any point in the supply chain, but what if it wasn't tampering, but outright sabotage designed to harm us. How many people would have to die before the fraud was detected? And once detected, how long would it take our people to trace it back to the source?"

"Maybe it's a test by the Chinese to see how far they can get," said Jesse. "When will we detect the counterfeit? Who will detect it? Will the meds make it into our pharmacies and hospitals? Will it be before deaths? Or after people have died, like the heparin incident?"

"You are describing a scary scenario," said Rachel. "People at the Pentagon aren't stupid. They have to know this."

"One would think" said Knight. "But sometimes short-term thinking and political games overshadow realities. The country is so divided. The impeachment mess, and the chaos and infighting created by this president, have us twisted in knots, at each other's throats, not really listening to each other."

"We're definitely not working together. The battle lines are drawn, Democrat or Republican," said Morgan.

"Knowing something and taking the necessary steps to ensure it doesn't happen are two different things," said Daniel. "In today's political climate, I'm not so sure what, if anything, is really being done to protect our forces."

The silence around the table was deafening.

"May I make a suggestion?" asked Moss.

Everyone around the table nodded and turned their attention to him.

"For now, let's not go there. Hold that issue in abeyance. It's too big. Let's focus locally. We've got a garage off Merrimac Trail filled with boxes of pharmaceuticals that are potentially dangerous for human consumption. We don't know anything about the guys who have them, or their ultimate destination."

"And we've got a guy who's been identified in a lineup who's selling tainted insulin at a flea market," added Knight.

"Do you have a picture of him?" asked Moss.

Knight pulled up a photo on his cell.

"Shit," said Moss. "This is one of the guys I saw at the garage, so we have our first solid connection." Moss stood and grabbed his plate. "These two issues are our priorities now. We can indulge in your Chinese checkers-biomedical-stealth warfare-what if game later, over beers."

Knight picked up his plate and headed for the kitchen, then stopped and turned back. "Counterfeit drugs are big business. Better than narcotics, because the penalties aren't as stiff. Misdemeanors mostly, more like a slap on the wrist, whereas opioids are felonies, which means big prison time."

"What do you think?" asked Morgan as she and Rachel cleaned up the dishes, leaving the men to continue their planning.

"What I think doesn't matter. What they do matters. So I'm more interested in what they're going to do."

"Good point." Morgan scraped food particles into the garbage. "Another thing I've found in my reading. Africa? Southeast Asia? You name a third world country, and I'll bet you any amount the drugs there are substandard. Like the ciprofloxacin Jesse had tested. There's an acronym, RoW, rest-of-world. It's the classification for medications going to places outside the United States, Canada, Europe, and Japan."

"I always assumed the medications we take here are the same as the medications everyone around the world gets," said Rachel.

"Wrong," said Morgan. "Want to know the funniest part?"

"Do I?"

"Many of the meds we take are actually manufactured in RoW countries. Big pharma has moved the majority of their plants to China and India, especially for generics. China makes most of the drugs' active ingredients and then ships them to India and other countries to be manufactured into capsules and pills and other delivery platforms."

"But the government has controls in place. The FDA. Right?"

"We hope. But let's face it, most of what the government does is shoddy at best. Bureaucrats can barely find their own asses with a flashlight and a road map. Look at the immigration mess at the Mexican border. Congress can't get out of its own way to address that crisis, and that's in their faces all day and night on TV. What makes you think they can do anything about contaminated drugs?"

Rachel's expression broadcast her thoughts about what Morgan was sharing. "This is so sad."

"I know. I've had a lot of sleepless nights since Jesse and I started this project." She blew out a breath. "I think I need dessert. Something sweet, or I'm going to cry."

"I've got just the thing." Rachel went to the refrigerator and pulled out an EDWARDS Turtle Crème Pie. "You get the coffee and I'll cut the pie."

"Okay, everyone," said Moss, tapping his water glass with a spoon. "First, thanks to Rachel for a fantastic dinner. Things have been moving pretty fast. Let's enjoy this delicious-looking pie and compare notes." He took a bite. "Tastes as good as it looks." He put down his fork. "What do we know? Facts. What do we think we know? Conjecture. And the ever-elusive, what don't we know."

"Ah, the basics—motive, means, opportunity," said Daniel, retrieving the white board from the closet.

Moss took the marker and created three columns, labeling each with one of the words, and adding a fourth column labeled "don't know."

"I'll make more coffee. Looks like we're in for a long night," said Rachel.

"Before we begin," said Moss, "I need to tell you about an encounter with an old friend that may have some bearing on what's happening here. Her name is Soraya Rousseau, although I suspect she's used a few other aliases in her career. The wicked witch of the west is Mother Theresa compared to Soraya. She's a ruthless, cunning, manipulative, heartless bitch."

"Interesting description," said Jesse.

"Destroy your enemies or be destroyed by them. There is no middle ground for her. Grew up on the streets of New Orleans."

"Sounds like my kind of gal," said Daniel. "And she plays into this how?"

"She approached me a few days ago, out of the blue. I haven't seen her for years. Had a lucrative proposition for me that centered on just what we're talking about—pharmaceuticals."

"What did she want you to do?" asked Knight.

"We haven't gotten around to the details yet, just said that a man with my skill set would be very helpful in her new venture."

"How did you leave it with her?" asked Jesse.

"Said I want to meet her partners because I don't trust her. I haven't heard back from her, but I can call her and see if she's still interested in my services."

"That might be worth doing," said Daniel. "Can't be a coincidence that she's talking pharmaceuticals, Jesse's caught up in tainted drugs, we've got a Congolese diplomat wandering around town, and you found a cache of what we think are contaminated drugs."

"And don't forget the guy I'm checking out selling expired insulin at the flea market," said Knight. "There is too much going on in sleepy little Williamsburg to think that somehow they're not all connected."

"What does she look like?" asked Jesse.

"Traffic-stopping figure, sexy, shiny long, dark hair, sultry dark eyes, sophisticated dresser, Eurasian features. Why do you ask?"

"Because a woman approached me at the Williamsburg Inn when I was tailing Matamba. Fits your description, but she had blue eyes and long blonde hair."

"Makeup, wig, colored contacts. Easy to do," said Morgan.

They got down to the nitty-gritty, filling the white board with details. It was past midnight when they broke. The white board was a mix of colors, squiggly lines, circles and connecting arrows.

"Okay,' said Daniel after several hours of brainstorming, "we each know what we need to do tomorrow. Let's touch base tomorrow night and see where we are."

"Do you think you'll be able to stop whatever is going on?" Rachel asked when Daniel crawled into bed.

"We better hope so, for the sake of countless people who may be in harm's way."

CHAPTER 20

Daniel was at his desk when Moss walked in.

"I need a favor."

"Anything."

"I need you to step back and take Knight with you."

"Do I get to ask why?"

Moss drummed his fingers on his thigh. "Because I'm going to go out on a limb and do Soraya's bidding, and I don't want to worry about getting shot accidentally by an overeager cop."

"So, you've got a plan?"

"A loosey-goosey one."

"You're making it up as you go?"

"Won't be the first time. I'm nothing if not adaptable."

"That's what worries me. Don't you think you'll need backup?"

"Yes, but Soraya will sniff out any cops lurking around, which will give her time to make her exit. And I want to take her down too."

"Sounds personal."

Moss smiled. "We know all these drug-related incidents are connected and I know Soraya is behind all of it."

"You've seen her in action before."

"Many times, and she always manages to slip away. I want that to end here. Don't worry. It'll be fun. You'll see."

"Sounds intriguingly dangerous. I can hardly wait."

"I'm surprised to hear from you," said Soraya when she joined Moss at Panera. "Pleasantly surprised." She looked around the small eatery. "How quaint. Is this where senior citizens spend their time?"

"Probably. No different than young singles meeting at a bar for drinks and to socialize. I thought morning coffee would keep us more focused on our conversation."

"How terribly boring. There was a time when you wouldn't have been caught dead in a place like this. Though their coffee is good."

"Business before pleasure."

"Does that mean pleasure isn't out of the question?" Soraya's hand reached across the table, gently covering his.

Moss rolled his eyes, but did not pull away.

"Your ostensible conversion to the straight and narrow is interesting, but I think I liked the rugged-for-hire you better."

"Why's that?"

"Do you believe in a God?"

"You're kidding, right? What kind of question is that?"

"A simple one."

"My belief system falls more along the lines of what I can see, feel, touch. All of which puts God out of the picture. And green is my favorite color."

"Glad to see that hasn't changed."

"What did your partners say about meeting?"

"When I told them about some of your escapades, they were quite impressed, but want to see you in action.

We've got some business to attend to, so if you're game…
and I do hope you are, because it would be so much fun to
work with you again…we can consider your involvement an
audition."

"Audition?"

"Let's get out of here." Soraya stood and headed for the
door, leaving her mess on the table. Moss picked everything
up, tossed it in the trash, and followed her. When they were
outside, she walked to the far end of the parking lot to the
dumpster where no cars were parked, turned, and faced him.

"Don't be offended by my associates' request. In their
experience, people rarely live up to the hype. And there's a
lot at stake." She took a step closer to him, fingering the
collar of his shirt, straying to his neck. "Like me, they're just
being cautious."

"So what are you into, and what do you need me for?"

"Security. Saturday night."

"A Saturday night special. Sounds like fun. And in
return?"

"Half a million."

"For one night's work? That is quite generous. Whatever
I'm securing must be quite valuable. Gold? Diamonds?"

"You don't need to know. Just do your job so we can do
ours. Make sure everything goes off without interference and
you will get your money."

"In dollars?"

"Of course in dollars. Unless you prefer something else."
Soraya stroked his cheek and pressed her body against his,
grinding her hips into him, feeling his response. "I might
consider some other forms of payment that would be more
pleasurable for both of us." Her hand found its way to his
groin and stroked him. "You seem ready."

"Maybe another time," He grasped her hand and twisted it
up to his chest, lightly kissing her fingertips. "For now, let's

do diamonds. Very transportable and they hold their value."

"It might be difficult to acquire that amount on such short notice."

"My dear, Soraya. You are nothing if not resourceful. Call one of your sheik friends. I'm sure they have an adequate stash close by."

"Does that mean you're in?"

"Point taken. Yes, but let me make a phone call, since I did have kind of a date."

"That older woman I saw you with?"

Moss's breath stalled. He let go of her hand and glared at her. "How long have you been following me?"

"Off and on for about a week. One can't be too careful. And I don't follow you everywhere. But I did see a woman hand you a beer while you were playing handyman the other day." Soraya tucked a wisp of hair behind her ear, enjoying that she'd caught him off guard. "She was pretty. A tad old for you, don't you think?"

"She's a friend. I'm helping her with a problem."

"Ah. Her son, the druggie. You know he's selling, right?"

Moss stepped back, sensing a foul mood descending on him. "I'm not sure this is going to work. I don't like being spied on."

"I wasn't spying. We've been out of touch for so long that I wanted to get a better feel for what you're doing here. Williamsburg isn't exactly a hotbed of intrigue." She reached to touch his arm, but he turned away. "And the sling that keeps going on and off. What's that about?"

"Flesh wound. I'm here recuperating and helping a friend build a dock for his canoe."

"Never remember you being the helpful type."

"People change."

"Yes...yes, they do. My only concern is whether your change is for the better or not."

"Don't worry your pretty little head. Just get the diamonds and I'll do my job. Where do I meet you?"

"I'll text you the information. Be ready by nine. Someone will pick you up."

"Ah. Fun and games in the dark."

"Is there any other way?" Soraya's step plastered her body against his again. She wrapped her arms around his neck and he returned the embrace with equal vigor, his hands resting on her neck, his fingers playfully moving along her hairline.

"Hmmmm," she purred. "Just like I remember." Her catlike smile as she turned to go jarred Moss. All she was missing was a long tail to whip around behind her.

Soraya's radar was on high alert as she got behind the wheel of her car. Something was off. She just wasn't sure what. The explanation about his sling and his flesh wound set off her bullshit meter. Bringing Moss into the game and trusting him again after all these years might prove to be her undoing.

Men were so easy to manipulate. It was her gift, and she'd been doing it for so long it came as second nature. Neither fully black, nor fully white, neither Asian nor Hispanic, a multi-racial ambiguity, she had roamed the streets of New Orleans turning tricks until a john got too rough. Within a week she had her revenge, an ice pick pierced his heart while he slept, but it forced her to flee. She secured passage on a cargo ship bound for Marseille, paying her way with favors to ensure the captain's comfort during the journey.

Marseille was a rough seaport, and Soraya learned how to survive on the streets, endearing herself to the city's mayor, who was only too happy to help her get settled in a villa on the hills overlooking the city, far away from his wife's prying eyes. She mastered her trade, pillow-talked her way into her clients' affairs, and sold bits and pieces of information to others for a small profit. She played them all, using her charms against them, pocketing the money they threw at her, plotting their demise.

And at a New Year's Eve celebration she saw her opportunity. A little of this, a little of that into the punch. She even playacted the role of victim to deflect suspicions. When it was over, the villa in Marseille was replaced by a larger one in Cannes, her profession became a distant memory, and a new career emerged, one where she showed herself to be more than a pretty face, and where she called the shots.

In her world there were no absolutes—nothing absolutely right or absolutely wrong. She made up her rules of play as her games unfolded, dabbling in drugs and guns, never picky about her customers. Nirvana struck when she chanced upon an article in the Financial Times about a pharmaceutical company in India playing fast and loose with manufacturing practices to the tune of a five million dollar fine from the European Union. If the company could pay that large a fine, how much money was the company actually making, and how?

Two days later found her at the Four Seasons Mumbai enjoying drinks and light conversation with Ajay Kumar. Three days later she was in his bed. Four days later she was a silent partner in his company, and through their pillow talk she quickly controlled the narrative, saved his company, his marriage, and his ass, all the while making her own planned sales and withdrawals.

C'est la vie. Or as they said in her native New Orleans, *laissez le bon temps rouler*, let the good times roll.

CHAPTER 21

Moss didn't see which car Soraya slipped into, but he positioned himself across from the lot's lone exit. He planned to follow her, thanks to the miniature tracking device he secured to the clasp of the gold necklace she always wore while he stroked her neck during their farewell embrace.

He opened the app on his cell phone, and the blinking red dot on his screen told him she was in the fire-engine red Mercedes stopped at the exit. He watched her turn onto Monticello heading west. She next turned onto Route 199 south, and then onto Brookwood Drive. Moss noted the Winery sign and wondered if she was meeting her partners for drinks. Her turn on Lake Powell Road pointed Moss in a different direction, and he slowed down so she wouldn't spot him in her rearview mirror. The airport. She was heading for the Williamsburg/Jamestown airport.

Soraya stayed to her left and drove down a rough dirt road adjacent to the airport with the runway on her right.

Moss pulled into the airport parking lot, grabbed his binoculars out of the glove compartment, and got out in time to watch her stop at the farthest end of the runway and back her car into the trees.

Moss already knew the beauty of general aviation airports was their anonymity. The formalities of flight plans, air traffic control, and reporting systems were nonexistent. Just a thirty-two hundred yard strip of asphalt in the middle of a field, surrounded by trees. His only question—who was she waiting for?

Time passed slowly. Waiting wasn't Moss's forte. The airport and Charley's restaurant, which was attached to the facility, had closed hours ago. Thinking ahead, he'd gotten himself a burger and fries to go before Charley's closed for the night. After eating, it was back to waiting, watching the hours tick by.

Midnight came and went. Then one o'clock. Moss checked to make sure Soraya's car was still in place. It was faint, but finally he heard the sound of an engine and suspected his patience was about to pay off. As soon as he heard engines clearly he got out of his car, put on his night vision goggles, and watched the glow of the plane's headlight get larger and larger on approach. *Sleek.* Moss knew his aircraft. The Challenger 300 banked and came in for a landing, rode the asphalt to the far end of the runway, and stopped.

And then another engine sound caught his attention. A black panel van with dimmed headlights came rumbling down the dirt road, past the airport parking lot. He watched it approach the far end and saw Soraya standing in front of her car, waving a small green-beamed flashlight. The truck pulled to within inches of her and stopped. Two men emerged, went to the back of the van, and began pulling out cartons, loading them on a dolly which, when full, they pushed out to the plane. Its cargo door opened, the cartons were loaded, and two more trips got the job done. The men got back in the van and left the way they came.

The plane's engines roared to life. It turned around, taxied to the opposite end of the runway, and took off.

In addition to Moss videoing the unloading of the van and the loading of the cargo onto the plane, he captured a photo of the plane's tail, recording the identifying numbers to send to Brett, who he was sure would be able to trace its flight path and uncover its ownership. When he looked back he could see Soraya watching the plane rise and disappear into the night sky. She made a call, probably signaling her partners that the shipment was on its way, then took one last look at the night sky, got back in her car, and left.

The was no need for Moss to rush to follow her. The night's activities were done, and the tracker beam showed the red dot coming his way as she left her hiding place.

Adam Knight sat at his desk, clutching his third cup of coffee and staring out the window, lost in thought. Folders detailing robberies, home invasions, and domestic abuse cases were piled high on his desk, but the case that caught his attention this morning wasn't one of his. He'd overheard night shift officers talking about a woman who slammed her car into the brick wall abutment opposite the Longhill Road exit of Route 199 last night. Fortunately, the child, who was securely strapped in the backseat, was bruised but would recover.

The victim's name stopped him dead in his tracks— Adelaide Lee. And the child? Lette. He blew out a breath. How much more pain could this little girl take? He reached for the phone.

"Debra, it's Adam. Sorry to bother you at work, but I just heard about Mrs. Lee and wanted to see how Lette was doing."

"So sad," said Debra. "I was on last night when they brought them in. Mrs. Lee died on the way here. The force of crash, her head hit the windshield and snapped her neck. The paramedics said she wasn't wearing her seat belt."

"Collisions with immovable objects like brick walls don't turn out well. How's Lette?"

"She's got a few cracked ribs, but fortunately she was buckled in tight. We've got her in the ICU. Not that she needs intensive care, but I thought it would be a good way to monitor her condition until we figure out what to do next."

"Smart." Adam swirled in his chair and pulled up the accident report on his computer. "I remember Mrs. Lee saying they didn't have family here."

"Lette said that when I was asking her about her relatives. But Adam, the more interesting thing she said was something about colored lights shining in the car just before the crash."

"Lights? You mean like the traffic light turning green."

"I don't think so. She was incoherent, rambling, but said something about Christmas lights. All twinkly. There was something about the way she said it. I don't think the officers who were asking her questions picked up on it."

"I've got the written report on the screen and it doesn't say anything about a green light in the car."

"That's what I'm saying. I was in the room, and I could tell by their expressions they thought she was talking gibberish because she was mentioning all the colors, red, then green, then blue. It was like she was running through a rainbow of colors."

"Think I'll stop by. Since she knows me from the insulin issue, maybe she'll be more open with me."

"That's what I was hoping you'd say. How much trouble will you get in with your fellow officers?"

"Not too much. I'll talk my way out of it. Don't worry. See you in about an hour."

Lette was sleeping when Adam entered her room, the little girl looking positively angelic while surrounded by machines beeping in a cacophony of tones. He sat down in the recliner and tried to make sense of the police report he just read about the accident, Debra's comments, and the now-orphaned little girl.

"Hi." Her soft voice pulled at his heartstrings.

"Hi, Lette. Remember me?"

"Sort of," she murmured. "You're the police guy."

"That's right. And here comes Dr. McKenna. Do you remember her?"

Debra came over to the bed, reached for the little girl's hand, and attached a blood oxygen meter to her finger.

"How are you feeling, sweetie?"

Lette looked around the room. "Where's my mommy?" Tears welled in her eyes.

Debra and Adam exchanged glances. "Honey, you and your mom were in a car accident last night. Do you remember what happened?"

"We were singing."

"Singing? That sounds like fun," said Debra.

"We always sing. Mama likes to sing. She's in the choir at church, and I'm in the children's choir."

"That's wonderful," said Adam. "Honey, Dr. McKenna said you told her you saw colored lights in the car."

"Yes. It looked like Christmas, and I started singing Jingle Bells." The little girl tried to stifle a yawn. "I'm tired. I want my m…"

She dozed off mid-sentence.

"We're going to have to tell her the next time she wakes up," said Adam.

"I know, and I'm dreading it," said Debra as she and Adam walked out of the room. "But it won't be the first time I've delivered awful news to a child, and thanks to my profession, I'm sure it won't be the last. Children experience loss and grief differently than adults do. I'm working on getting counseling ready for her, and I'm meeting with the hospital's chaplain in an hour to get his thoughts."

"I'm stuck on the colored lights thing. Christmas could just be the reflection from the traffic light at that corner."

"True, but she mentioned blue and purple to me last night, and those aren't traffic light colors."

"But they are laser colors."

"What are you thinking?"

"That someone was shining a laser into the car and temporarily blinded Mrs. Lee just as she was pressing on the gas. It startled her. She hit the pedal hard and slammed into the brick wall."

"Think it was kids playing around?"

"If it had been during the day or earlier in the evening I'd say yes. But the police report said this happened just after midnight. We did a lineup last week and arrested the guy she fingered." Adam thought about it for a moment. "Where was she going at that hour? And when did she get a car? When she was here she said she didn't have a car. Remember?"

"She could have borrowed it from a neighbor. But the time thing has me curious. I'm also wondering where she was going. Their home is in the opposite direction, and there aren't any stores off Longhill. It's more residential."

"Good point." Adam looked at Lette. "Too many questions that I'm afraid we may never be able to answer."

CHAPTER 22

"Sure would like to know more about the people who live here," said Knight. He'd called Daniel and told him about Mrs. Lee, then asked to meet close to the house on Merrimac Trail where Moss found the pharmaceutical stash. "All the records tell us is the owner's name, Ralph Engels. The place looks deserted. Be great to get a look inside."

"I can do that," said Moss.

"Legally?"

"Of course legally. I'm the epitome of legally." Moss's sly smile made Knight sorry he asked. "Hang loose here. If anything changes, call me." Moss left Daniel and Knight, got back in his own car, and drove off.

"Do you know what he's going to do?" asked Knight.

"Haven't a clue," said Daniel.

About twenty minutes later Daniel nudged a sleepy Knight. "Showtime."

They watched as a bald man in a charcoal gray suit, red tie, and crisp white shirt, a book in his hand, walked up to the front door.

"Twenty bucks says he doesn't get in," said Knight.

"Oh, ye of little faith. You're on."

Although they couldn't see who answered the door, Moss's gestures let them know he was deep into his spiel. The storm door opened, and Moss disappeared into the house in under two minutes.

"Amazing." Knight dug into his pocket and pulled out a twenty. "Don't spend it all in one place."

Daniel laughed. "Never bet against a man like Moss. I learned that a long time ago. He's like a dog with a meaty bone. Driven, relentless, determined to get his prize."

"I'll remember that."

The woman who answered the door introduced herself as Sally Engels. She was a matronly, grandmother type with thin lips, close-set tired eyes, and a double chin that fused into her neck. Moss guessed her to be in her fifties. Her dull, gunmetal gray hair peppered with white streaks was pulled back in a bun at the nape of her neck. She wore no makeup and her dress was a simple flowered A-line with a high neck and long sleeves. Sensible shoes adorned her feet.

"Thank you for taking the time to pray with me, sister."

"Bless me, Reverend. It is so kind of you to visit." She pulled off her apron and smoothed the front of her dress. "May I get you coffee? I've got some fresh pecan pie cooling, and I'd love to share a piece with you."

"That would be splendid." Moss's ever-observant eyes wandered around the room, from left to right, making mental notes of objects present and those missing. Then he followed her into the kitchen.

"We're new to the neighborhood and haven't decided on a church yet. It's been a while since I've been to prayers."

"We can pray together while I'm here."

"That would be wonderful. Please sit down." She poured coffee and sliced into the pie. "My husband, Ralph, isn't a religious man. He'll go to church with me occasionally, but that's as far as it goes."

"And yet your home is resplendent with articles of faith," said Moss, who'd noted the several crosses and statues as he walked from the front door to the kitchen.

"Old habits. They bring me peace."

"That's wonderful. In these turbulent times, finding simple ways to be at peace is a blessing." Moss sipped his coffee. "May I ask what type of work your husband does?"

"He's in shipping. Don't ask me what," she giggled like a schoolgirl. "He doesn't tell me much about his work, but it's why we moved here. He's a good man. We want for nothing, and I'm able to tithe at church."

"That's a blessing in and of itself. Helping the less fortunate."

"We weren't blessed with children, and Ralph is allergic to dogs and cats, so I always spend a lot of time involved with my church. That's what I'm hoping to do here."

"And we welcome your participation. Ours is a warm, welcoming community." Moss reached out his hand and put it on top of hers. "I'll have Mary Lou Barton give you a call. She runs our outreach ministry. Perhaps that's a committee you'd like to join."

"Oh, Reverend, that would be wonderful."

"Mrs. Engels, this pie is spectacular. You must make it for the annual bake sale."

"It would be a privilege, Reverend."

Moss took another forkful. "Shipping is such detail-oriented work. If I even think about all the things I use every day, my head spins from how to keep track of it all. I'll bet your husband is good with computers. You know, to keep track of deliveries."

"I don't rightly know. Ralph works out of the garage in the back. Men are always coming and going. Picking up boxes and dropping off more boxes. My stars, I don't know how he keeps track of it all."

Moss finished his pie and took his dirty plate and coffee cup to the sink. He stared out the kitchen window at the garage. He could see the second garage partially hidden behind it.

"Is there another home that backs up on your property? I see another garage back in the woods."

"No, that's ours too. It's one of the reasons Ralph wanted this house."

"It's nice that you each have a garage for your car."

"Heavens, no. I don't drive. Ralph takes me for groceries, the doctor, or wherever I need to go. And with the internet, most things I need get delivered. I'm sure I keep the UPS man and Amazon Prime in business."

Moss felt a creepy sensation crawl up his spine. Something wasn't right with this woman. Who doesn't drive these days?

"I have to admit this house wasn't my favorite of the ones we looked at, but I didn't get much say in the matter. Business comes first. The second garage is Ralph's business."

"With all that inventory, I hope you have a top-notch security system in place. There have been a few home invasions and robberies in the area over the past few months."

"My stars! Thanks so much for telling me that. I don't think we have any type of security system yet. As I said we just moved here a few months ago. But I'll be sure to pass it on to Ralph. He's out of town for a few days at a distributors' meeting."

"Please don't think I'm being nosy, but we have a large congregation. Over five hundred families. What type of products does he distribute? Maybe some of our families can become customers."

"Some sort of drugs. Not the bad kind. The good kind that help people like aspirin, and antibiotics, and…well, I don't rightly know what else, but you get the idea."

"Yes. Yes, I do. That's wonderful. So many people rely on the pharmaceutical industry for their very lives."

"Yes. That's what I meant when I said Ralph was a good man. I know he gives away a lot of medicines to those less-fortunate souls who find themselves in dire straits."

Moss noted the chiming of a clock. "Mrs. Engels, I've taken enough of your time." They walked to the front door. Moss reached out his hand and held it over her head. "Dear Lord, bless this woman, Sally Engels, your child. Keep her in your loving arms. Protect her from harm and deliver her the best of your gifts, good health and long life. In the name of Jesus Christ. Amen."

Tears filled Mrs. Engels eyes. "No minister has ever blessed me alone. Thank you so much. I'll see you in church on Sunday for sure."

Five minutes later, Knight saw Moss's car pull up behind his and Moss slipped into the back seat.

"Spill," said Knight. "How did you know there was a woman there and that she'd let you in?"

"Saw a cross hanging in the kitchen window the other night, which told me to go the religious route. Took my chances that someone would be home, and I was hoping for a female. Women are easy marks, especially religious ones."

"What did you learn?" asked Daniel.

Moss handed over his cell phone. "Listen for yourselves."

They replayed the conversation twice while they drove back to Daniel's house. And a third time when Jesse arrived.

"Now what do we do?" asked Jesse. "I know what I'd like to do—beat the shit out of Ralphie—but I suspect you two have a better idea."

"We have to catch him with the goods," said Daniel. "Make it a slam-dunk case against him and try to flip him to point us to the higher-ups."

"I agree," said Knight. "Ralph and his crew are lowlifes. We want the guys in charge, the people running the operation."

"And how do you propose we do that?" asked Jesse.

"We need someone on the inside to roll over on the higher-ups," said Daniel. "Bait and trap."

"And who's gonna do that?" asked Jesse.

"I think I can help. Gotta make a phone call." Moss left the room but returned quickly. "No answer. Guess I have to pay a face-to-face visit. I'll call you tomorrow."

CHAPTER 23

A light drizzle and north wind whipping through the trees made for a dismal night. Moss kept calling Howie's cell, but there had been no answer for hours.

"Hey Sara," said Moss when she answered the door. "Is Howie here?"

"No. I haven't seen him all day. Want to come in and wait?"

"No. If you talk to him, let him know I'm looking for him." He turned to go.

He was different, standoffish, thought Sara. Something was wrong. "Moss?"

He knew what was coming and turned back to face her.

"I can tell he's in some kind of trouble. What's going on?"

"There's a complication, one I can't ignore." He touched her cheek.

"I wouldn't expect you to ignore anything." His tone and probing stare riled her, and she stepped away from him, not wanting him to feel any obligation because they'd slept together.

"He's…There were drugs in the storage locker Howie bought. Not opioids. Medications. All different types. Cartons of them. The one carton I managed to open before

182

he stopped me had boxes of amoxicillin in it. Expired amoxicillin. They got moved." Moss pulled her to him and wrapped his arms around her. "Howie's involved in something really shady. And the sooner I figure out how deeply he's involved, the sooner I can help him break free."

"I'm sorry, Moss." She broke free of his embrace. "As his mother, I probably shouldn't say this, but the boy's got shit for brains."

"I'm the one who's sorry. I told you I'd try to help him. But addiction… It's a killer. A Jekyll and Hyde experience. Up one moment, down the next. Economic impact, familial impact, health impact. People think it will never happen to them, but no one's immune."

"I know," said Sara. "When I broke my ankle last year, my doctor prescribed Percocet. The prescription was for sixty pills. Sixty. Not ten and then call my office if you're still in pain. But sixty right off the bat."

"How many did you use?"

"Five."

"And the rest?"

"They were in my medicine cabinet, but I noticed a few were missing after Howie paid me a visit last spring, so when he showed up this time I hid them." Sara shrugged.

"Did you confront him?"

"I asked him about the pills, but he swore a blue streak he didn't take any."

"You think he's lying?"

"Were his lips moving?" Sara laughed. "He lies all the time. Part of his persona."

"Not an endearing quality."

The grandfather clock in the foyer chimed ten.

"Sure you don't want to come in and wait? He should be here soon. No matter what condition he's in, he somehow makes it back here nearly every night."

"Thanks, but I'll catch up with him later. Just let him know I stopped by."

Moss got back in his car and drove down the street, parking in front of a neighbor's house, giving him a clear view of Sara's driveway. He'd be able to see when Howie showed up. Staking out Sara's house waiting for Howie to return was not Moss's idea of fun, but it had to be done. He cracked the driver's side window to clear the thickening condensation inching across the windshield.

An hour later Moss saw his target pull into the driveway. Howie didn't get out right away. Moss could see him bopping and weaving behind the wheel, white earbuds hanging from his ears, his eyes on his phone.

Moss laughed to himself as he watched the fool, oblivious to his surroundings. The concept of situational awareness was lost on this boy. He'd never be a top player, just a low-level runner, very replaceable. Not worth much effort, but Moss was sure he could lead them to the higher-ups if he could be convinced to cooperate. And Moss was a powerful persuader.

Moss walked up to the car and rapped on the passenger side window. Howie jumped, dropping his phone and hitting his head on the roof of the car.

Howie rolled down the window. "You scared the shit out of me. What the hell are you sneaking up on me for?"

"It's showtime, kid. How good an actor are you?"

"Something's off," said Debra when Adam answered his phone.

"What are you talking about?"

"With Lette. I told her about her mother dying in the

crash but she didn't get upset. Not like I would have expected. She didn't cry. Not one tear."

"You said it yourself, children experience grief differently than adults."

"I know they do, but Lette acted like I told her we ran out of red Jell-O. And the more I think about it, other than when you were here, she hasn't asked where her mom is at all. Something's not right."

"Maybe her mom's death hasn't settled in yet."

"That could be, but I asked a child psychologist friend who's on staff to meet with Lette and do a quick evaluation. Nothing formal. Jillian uses art therapy in her work, and since Lette isn't very verbal I thought drawing might be a way to help her express herself."

"It sounds like your concerns got worse."

"You need to see the pictures Lette has been drawing and tell me what you think."

"I'm not exactly trained to do that."

"I don't think it's going to take much training."

"They're that disturbing?"

"You tell me."

"Okay. I'm on until four. I'll swing by the hospital on my way home."

"Thanks. And to show you my appreciation, I'll take you to dinner at Giuseppe's. My treat."

"Works for me. See you later."

For two days Moss, Jesse and Daniel had been doing routine surveillance on the Engels place. They scheduled their visits at prime times, but never saw Ralph Engels coming or going. The big surprise came on day three, when Moss watched Sally Engels drive away in a black Lexus

SUV. And the photographs he took of her with a telephoto lens revealed a strikingly different-looking person than the homely woman he originally met.

"That bitch lied to me." Moss grinned when he shared the photos with Daniel.

"What are you going to do?" asked Daniel.

"I think a return visit is in order. Confront her. See what happens."

Moss parked a few houses down, switched off the engine and stared at the Engels house. He'd driven by twice, saw a light in the living room the second time he passed. Someone was home, hopefully Sally. He blew out a breath, changed his shirt, pulled a bible out of the glove compartment, and traced his fingers over the embossed gold letters. He put it back in the glove compartment and got out of the car.

When she finally came to the door she didn't look happy to see him, but recovered quickly, plastering a sickly sweet smile on her face.

"Mrs. Engels, how delightful to see you again."

"Bless your heart, Reverend. What a pleasant surprise. Come in. Come in." She stood back as Moss entered. "Let me make some coffee. I've got peach cobbler if you're interested."

"Please don't go to any trouble." Moss followed her into the kitchen. "But if your cobbler is even half as good as your pecan pie, I can hardly pass it up."

"It's nice to see you, but I'm confused. Please tell me what's going on. I know ministers make house calls, but rarely two in as many days. Did something happen to Ralph? Is he hurt?"

"Mrs. Engels, I feel I have betrayed your trust and I am so sorry."

"I don't understand."

"I came to you under false pretenses the other day.

I'm not a man of the cloth. And now I must confess my trespass and make amends."

"I still don't understand. You're not a minister?"

Something in her eye told Moss she already knew he wasn't who he had claimed to be during his first visit, but if she was going to play dumb, he'd go along.

"It's about your husband, Ralph. I fear he has become embroiled in some shady business dealings that can bring great harm to many innocent people."

"Are you the police?"

"No, but I often work with the police. I'm a private investigator working on a case. Ralph has come to my attention and I need your help."

"My help? What could I possibly do to help you?"

"You said your husband is out of town. Tell me, when is he coming home?"

"Tonight. He said he'd be home for supper."

Moss thought about that for a moment. "I may be out of line here, but do you happen to have a key to the lock on the garage back in the woods?"

"His office? Why on earth do you want to..." Sally Engels bit her upper lip. "No. Don't answer that. Ralph's no saint. Whatever he's into... What can I say? I'm not much to look at. Lord knows why he married me. But he's a good husband. Faithful to me. At least I think he's faithful, and if he's cheating, at least he doesn't do it in front of me, so what I don't know for a fact can't hurt me." She dried her hands on her apron though they weren't wet. "The key's on a hook by the back door."

"And just to be clear," said Moss, "there isn't a security system. No cameras, video recorders?"

"Not that I know about. But then I never go back there. Ignorance is bliss. Can't get upset about things you don't know about."

"That's true. So I have your permission to look around."

"Yes. But I don't want to know what you find."

"I'll do my best." Moss headed for the back door, took the key off the hook, and, after a short pause, turned back to her. "Is there anything you can tell me about Ralph's business?"

"Nothing more than I told you last time. He's in distribution. He moves stuff around. Cartons of stuff. Drugs, but not the bad kind."

"Is there any set schedule to his shipments?"

"Men show up every few days in small trucks or vans. Sometimes they unload boxes and then a few days later a different truck comes and takes boxes away."

"Is it the same men?"

"For the drop-off yes, but different men come to take the stuff away."

"Have you ever talked to any of the men? Could you give us a description?"

"Not really. I go about my business when they're here. I know Ralph doesn't like it when I ask too many questions." Sally touched the side of her cheek.

"Does he hit you?"

She turned away. "He...he has. But not lately. Things are going really well here. There were a lot of problems where we used to live. It's why we moved."

"And where was that?"

"Hampton. I liked living there. We were close to town, and in the warm weather I'd walk into town and ride the carousel. It's an antique, you know."

"I didn't know that."

"Yes. Made me feel like a schoolgirl again. Whirling around. The calliope music. Oh my, I could go on and on. But you don't want to hear from a silly woman reminiscing about the past."

Moss grinned. "Now, Sally, we both know you're not a silly woman." Slowly he reached into his pocket, pulled out several photos, and proceeded to lay them down on the table in front of Sally, one at a time.

Sally raised her eyebrow. "You've been spying on me."

"Not spying. Just confirming a feeling. Something about you didn't play for me, and I don't like loose ends.

"Now what?"

"That, my dear, depends on you."

CHAPTER 24

The next day Moss, Daniel, and Jesse found themselves following Ralph Engels. He'd led them through Lowes and Walmart, down Richmond Road for a burger stop at McDonalds, and now they were approaching Colonial Williamsburg.

"We could lose him," said Jesse as the guy's car turned into the two-hour parking lot off South Henry Street.

"Bigger problem," said Daniel. "It's Thursday and not that crowded. He could spot us."

"Not to worry. I brought clothes. Check the bag on the floor behind my seat." said Moss. "Shirts, hats, a few wigs, glasses, everything you need to effect a quick disguise."

"Jesse, get out here and keep him in sight," said Daniel, stopping suddenly and ignoring the blaring horn of the car behind him. "I'll park in the lot behind the Craft House. You can text where he's heading so Moss and I can catch up."

"Good idea." Jesse grabbed a green William and Mary Tribe sweatshirt, black horn-rimmed glass, and hopped out. He stood at the ticket window and could see Ralph Engels parking his car and talking on his cell. He saw Daniel and Moss take positions, one in front of Barnes and Noble, the other on the top step of the Craft House.

"He's coming in your direction, Daniel, carrying a white plastic bag," said Jesse as Engels took the path towards DoG street.

"I'm heading into the store. I can see him through the door."

Moss joined Jesse and they walked to a bench in front of the Cheese Shop, assuming the posture of two bored husbands waiting for their wives.

"He's right outside," said Daniel, "at one of the tables. Another guy just joined him. There are two white bags on the table now."

"See him," said Moss. "We're moving closer."

Moss poked Jesse and they both got up. They repositioned themselves at an empty table outside the DoG Street Pub, not worried about a server bugging them to order food because outside service was only available on weekends. They had a clear view of Engels, who was now engaged in a conversation with the other person at his table.

"Daniel, we've got a problem," said Moss.

"What?"

"The guy sitting with Engels? It's Sara's son, Howie. That little pissant lied to me. Said he was going to help Sara clean out the garage today."

"Damn." Daniel peered out the store window. "You're right." He took off his cap and rubbed his head. "Shit. He knows all of us. We can't approach him. Let me call Knight."

It took a few minutes for Daniel to get back to Moss. "Knight's got an officer in the area. He's sending him my way. Has Howie moved?"

"Not yet," said Jesse.

Jesse and Moss stayed put, playing with their cell phones, watching the two men laughing and talking like old friends.

Moss spoke into his cell. "Howie's on the move. Took Engels' white bag. On DoG Street, heading for Bruton

Parish church. Blue baseball cap. Blue windbreaker with white stripe across the chest."

"Copy that," said Daniel. "Knight's guy is with me, so he'll follow Howie."

Then Moss turned to Jesse, who was sitting next to him at the table.

"Did you see that?"

"What?"

"The switch."

"Didn't see anything."

"Engels sat down at the table and put down his bag. The other guy, Howie, joined him, also putting down a white bag. Only when Howie got up, he took Engels' bag."

"Shit, how'd you see that?"

"Tradecraft. It's the classic swap move. You see it all the time in movies, only it's usually a briefcase. Unless you're watching closely, you'd never notice it." Moss stood. "Come on. Our guy's moving. Let's go."

Moss's cell beeped.

"Howie's been detained. Xanax in the bag."

"Copy." Moss shook his head. "We're following Engels. Let's see where he goes next."

Next turned out to be home. Moss saw him get a warm, welcoming kiss from Sally before the door closed.

"We're done. Jesse and I are off to Opus for beers. Want to join us?"

"No," Daniel said "Think I'll head home for a quiet night. I've got a feeling all hell is about to break loose. Think a quiet night is called for."

"Now that is one hot-looking woman," said Jesse when he and Moss walked out of Opus 9.

"Yes. And dangerous."

"You know her?"

"Unfortunately. And you said you met her, too. Blonde, blue eyes, looking for the Kimball."

"No. Can't be the same woman."

Soraya walked towards them. Her hips swayed gently in skin-tight leggings, and her long, dark hair moved with the light breeze.

"Evening, Moss." She went up on her toes and brushed Moss's cheek with a kiss, making sure to push her voluptuous breasts against him. "I do declare, you get more handsome each time I see you. And who is your friend?"

"Jesse Sinclair, meet Soraya Rousseau."

"*Enchanté*." Soraya extended her hand. "Moss always has such interesting friends. What type of work do you do, Mr. Sinclair?"

Moss held up his hand to preempt any reply. "What do you want, Soraya?"

"I was in the neighborhood. Saw you sitting on the patio. Didn't want to intrude, so I thought I'd wait out here."

Jesse couldn't take his eyes off her, her intense dark eyes held him under their spell, lustrous hair she tossed about, eyelashes batting, the sway of her hips as she spoke, each move seductive, purposeful, designed to lure men under her spell. And the pulse between Jesse's legs told him it was working. Soraya Rousseau was a force to be reckoned with, and one intimidating woman.

"Well, goodbye then, since you don't want to intrude," said Moss.

"So rude. Unbecoming even for you, Moss."

"If you have something to say, please say it."

"I wanted to tell you our plans have taken shape and we'll be requiring your security services for tomorrow night. Will that fit into your schedule?"

"Yes. I'm free and can be available." He opened his phone and pulled up notes. "The account for my fee, payable in advance is…" He stopped talking. "Aren't you going to write this down?"

"Don't you remember I have a photographic memory? I see words and once I see them, I don't forget them."

"Right." He twisted his cell phone so Soraya could see the account number. "I get immediate notification when deposits clear this account. As long as everything goes smoothly on this end," he wiggled his cell, "I'll be at your disposal."

"Excellent." She held out her hand to Jesse. "It's been a pleasure meeting you, Mr. Sinclair. Perhaps we can do business one day. I'm sure my life story would fascinate your readers."

Soraya got into her car and left. They watched her car circle the rotary and drive away.

"You certainly know some interesting people." Jesse rubbed his chin. "You're right. She is the woman who stopped me when I was following Matamba. Same sultry voice."

"A ploy, but it tells us that she and Matamba are in cahoots."

"How does she know I have readers? You stopped me before I told her what I did."

"Soraya has ways. She, like you, is a researcher. She does her homework. And before you get too interested, you might think of her as a revenge angel."

"Revenge angel? Those terms seem mutually exclusive."

"Ah. So they are. Not sure how else to describe her. She feeds on revenge for even the tiniest slight. And she does it smiling all the way. Her victims never see it coming, which is why she's so successful. And she leaves nothing to chance, which usually means no loose ends. No witnesses."

"That's got to make you nervous, especially since it sounds like you two are planning something."

"Do I look nervous?"

"No."

"She thinks I'm on her side. And for her it's business not personal." Moss thought for a moment. "Until it becomes personal, and then all bets are off. She's an exotic sociopath, so if I were you I'd stop drooling and keep my distance."

"What's happening tomorrow night?"

"All in good time, my friend. All in good time."

Soraya stopped the car after a block and pounded the steering wheel like a spoiled child who'd dropped her ice cream cone. Her instincts were right. Moss had converted. He was no longer trustworthy and had to be removed from any plans. Maybe removed permanently.

She picked up her cell and hit the five on speed dial.

"It's cleanup time, darling."

"What do you mean?"

"We have a slight problem requiring a change of plans. I need you here in Williamsburg to handle things."

"*Ce que les choses?* What things?"

"We have a few loose ends that need to disappear. An old friend has disappointed me, and you know how I hate being disappointed."

"*Ç'est malheureux.* How unfortunate. I will text you when I arrive."

"Thank you so much."

Soraya leaned her forehead against her hands, which were still clutching the steering wheel, and sighed loudly. So much promise destroyed so quickly. She had big plans for her post-job reunion with Moss. But seeing him with the reporter ended everything.

She took a deep breath, composed herself, started the car, and drove to the Inn. Her walk across the lobby was more reminiscent of a truck driver than a seductress. She pounded the elevator button, not once, not twice, but repeatedly—until it finally arrived. When she got to her suite, she poured herself a drink, kicked off her shoes, and threw herself onto the sofa.

"*Merde.*"

Adam's expression broadcasted his concern when he approached Debra outside the ER triage room.

"What's wrong?" asked Debra.

"We got a hit on Lette's DNA."

"It's in the system?"

"Yes. NCMEC. National Center for Missing and Exploited Children. Missing since 2014. Mrs. Lee wasn't Lette's mother."

"Whoa." Debra rubbed her forehead. "Who was she?"

"Who knows? There was a familial match. Maybe an aunt or something." He handed Debra a file.

"This says Lette went missing five years ago. She must have some repressed memory of someone else, which might explain why she wasn't devastated when I told her that her mother died. Or the person we assumed was her mother."

"The woman said they were from Arkansas, so I've got someone searching records from that part of the country. Hopefully we'll get a hit."

CHAPTER 25

"Jesse, you can't publish your story until we wrap these guys up," said Daniel when he and Rachel served dessert on the deck.

"Why's that?"

"Panic. People will panic. They'll look at the medicines they take and wonder if they should take them. We can't have that."

"How does this happen?" asked Rachel. "I don't understand. Isn't the FDA in charge of protecting the public from tainted drugs?"

"Yes, but the FDA is limited in its reach. It's a humongous bureaucracy and can't be everywhere all the time, although we like to think it can," said Daniel. "No government agency can be everywhere. Not the CIA, FBI, NSA. And, unfortunately, not the FDA."

"I remember during my senior internship with a now-defunct Richmond newspaper who mistakenly chose not to hire me full time," said Morgan, a wicked smile on her face, "a drug company warehouse was robbed. It was big news because they got away with a lot of Advair inhalers. About a year later some of the stolen inhalers showed up at a few local pharmacies in some of the poor neighborhoods. The police went in, arrested the owners for buying and reselling stolen goods, and pulled the stuff off the shelves. But I'll bet there are more inhalers out there and unsuspecting people are still buying them at discount prices. And by now, the medicine has expired."

"You're describing a very dangerous scenario," said Rachel.

"The system is failing people on so many levels," said Morgan. "Costs are skyrocketing, forcing people to go outside traditional channels to get the medications they need."

"I never really thought about it, but several of my neighbors order their medications from the internet," said Rachel. "They say they're less expensive."

"They probably are, but they don't know where the meds are coming from and the quality may not be the same," said Morgan.

"At some point, we will publish this story," said Jesse. "People have a right to know what's happening to our drug supply. And who's asleep at the wheel."

"But isn't that the quintessential question?" asked Rachel. "What is actually happening?"

"Morgan and I are uncovering gigantic holes in the system. The FDA, such as it is, can't police a system with so many foreign suppliers who are protected from prosecution by archaic laws designed for a time long gone. Globalization is the enemy here."

"What we find needs to go up the chain so leadership can put systems in place to mitigate any damage," said Daniel.

"Leadership? You mean like Congress?" chided Jesse. "Those fools can't get out of their own way. A customer outcry can achieve in months what it would take years for the petty, sniveling bastards in Congress to accomplish."

"What needs to happen is simple," said Daniel. "Big pharma needs to step up, forgo some profits, and bring manufacturing back to the US, under watchful eyes and more direct control of the FDA."

"Forgo profits?" laughed Rachel. "Like that will ever happen."

"Then we must force the issue," said Morgan. "Exactly what we want our article to do. Companies don't like bad press, and even big pharma is vulnerable to millions of customers clamoring for made-in-America drugs. If enough people start screaming about imported meds, demanding reasonable prices for both branded and generic drugs made here…"

"It could get really ugly," said Rachel.

"Better ugly than dead," said Jesse.

The knock on the door repeated itself twice before Matamba got off the bed and went to look through the peephole. He saw nothing but an empty hall.

He headed back to the bed, but the knock came again. Without thinking or looking, he opened the door. Two burly men each grabbed one of his arms and pushed him back into the room, forcing him into the chair at the small breakfast table.

"What is the meaning of this outrage?" He started to stand but was forcefully pushed back down.

"Take a breath and have a seat," said one of the men. "Someone will be here shortly to explain everything."

"You have no right to detain me, let alone arrest me."

"I'm not arresting you. They are." The man pointed to two men who were entering the room. Both wore dark suits, red ties, and white shirts. "Or rather, they are detaining you, *and* deporting you."

"Without so much as a hearing? What is the reason?"

"Don't know. Don't care."

"You insolent little twerp. Do you know who I am? Who I represent?"

"Same answer. Don't know. Don't care."

When the two white-bread-looking men reached the table, each one showed his credentials. "I'm Tobias Lent," said the taller man. "State Department. You'll be coming with us."

"And if I refuse?"

"Really? It's been a long day. Do you really want to make a scene?"

"I know my rights."

"Any rights you may have had existed before the Patriot Act. Now all you've got is a phone call," said Lent.

"Which you can make once we get to Richmond," said the other official. "And I probably could find several little-known rules that would allow me to deprive you of that, so don't piss me off."

When Knight arrived, the firemen were hauling their heavy hoses back to the trucks.

"What happened?" asked Knight when he approached the fire chief.

"The place blew up. Not much left. The arson guys may be able to tell us something about how the fire started, but they've got their work cut out for them. My guess is someone cut the gas line."

"Anyone inside?"

"We found one body. Looks like she was thrown free in the blast. She's over there with the ME." He pointed to the far side of the scene.

Knight walked around the debris toward the ME. The smell of burned wood and smoke filled his lungs and he started coughing. When he reached the ME, who was down on one knee examining a charred body, he was handed a bottle of water by a passing firefighter.

"Thanks." He uncapped it and took a huge gulp. "What have you found?"

"Blunt force trauma. Someone hit our victim with something hard. Fractured her skull. The explosion and fire were overkill, but fortunately she was thrown far enough away so we have a witness. A dead witness, but dead bodies do tell tales."

Merrimac Trail was closed to traffic in both directions by the time the fire department finished storing their hoses and made preparations to leave. The fire was out, but one truck would stay behind to put out any flare-ups that might occur.

Ralph watched from the mini mart gas station down the street, close enough to see the action, but far enough away that no one working the scene would consider his interest suspicious. He stood with others, mostly tradesmen, enjoying a burrito and a Coke. His momentary sadness at Sally's horrific death was eased by the knowledge that it was her or him, and Ralph was a survivor.

His cell vibrated in his pocket and he walked away from the crowd. Blocked number.

"Engels."

"My instructions were followed?"

"Precisely." Ralph knew better than to improvise. "The Sally loose end is no more."

"Fabulous. Did you find the package I left for you?"

"Yes. Is it clean?"

"Untraceable. A ghost gun."

"Any particular target in mind?"

"You'll know him when you see him."

"I think I already have. Big guy. Tough."

"Make it look like he got in the way of a bullet meant for someone else."

"How about the reporter? We missed him at the library."

"Don't remind me."

"How about a twofer? If it was up to me—"

"Then it's a good thing it's not up to you. No twofer. It would arouse too much suspicion. There will come another time to take care of Mr. Sinclair."

"Your wish is my command."

"Just see that it's done."

Jesse walked out to get the mail. Once back inside with the door closed, he headed for the kitchen, but stopped at the doorway.

Morgan was about to say something, but he held his finger to his lips in the shhhh motion. Without a word, he turned and went back out the front door, this time paying attention to his surroundings.

"What's up?" asked Morgan as she followed him outside.

"Black SUV…parked down the street…two guys inside…looked like they were having coffee." His whispered voice broadcast caution.

"And?"

"Morgan? Black SUV? Just hanging out on our street? Doesn't that seem odd to you?"

"Yes. I guess it does. What should we do?"

"Let's get a patrol car over here. Could easily take five, ten minutes. If they're still here, the police can approach them."

"But what's the point of watching my house? You gave the vials back. What else is there?"

"Hold that thought. Stay here." Jesse walked back inside,

came back out a few minutes later with his Go bag, grabbed her hand, and pulled her into the foyer. He put his finger to his lips and made the shhhh gesture again. A silent communication, acknowledged by a barely perceptible nod.

"What are your plans for the day, Morgan?" He tapped his ear with his fingertip and rolled his other hand in a small circular motion to signal that he wanted her to talk, sharing innocuous information about her plans. He took a wand out of his pack, and as she spoke, he walked through the rooms slowly, waving the wand up to the ceiling and then down to the floor. He stopped at a spider plant that hung above her kitchen sink and showed her the monitor screen, which was registering at its highest level.

Morgan grabbed a post-it and pencil and wrote, *Now what?*

He wrote back, *Keep talking. Normal conversation. Nothing revealing.*

Moss chuckled to himself. His years of military service and covert operations made him keenly aware of all the things that could go wrong. There was the plan...and then there was the shit that actually happened.

Adaptability was key. It was how he got his name, Moss, as in that stuff a rolling stone doesn't gather. His special forces buddies always marveled at his ability to read the terrain, shift gears, respond in the moment, overcome obstacles.

His cell rang. He looked at the caller ID and smiled.

"Hey, Brett. How are the alligators?"

"You know Florida. Down here we keep 'em as pets."

"Yeah. Until they eat your puppy. Then you take revenge. Cook 'em up and make boots out of their skin."

"Nice talk. Anyway, I pulled this up and thought you'd be interested," said Brett. "Ralph Engel, convicted felon, former military, BCD. I've sent you his picture to make sure it's the same guy you're tracking up there."

"It's him," said Moss after looking at the photo. "BCD? Bad conduct discharge? He got the big chicken dinner, huh? What'd he do?"

"Decked his lieutenant. No jail time for that, but the Army cut him loose."

"He must have known someone important to avoid winding up in Leavenworth."

"After that he did five years of a seven-year sentence for armed robbery."

"Looks like he's a magnet for trouble."

CHAPTER 26

"Have a seat, Mr Engels," said Knight as he held open the door to the interrogation room. Can I get you something to drink? Coffee? A soda?"

"I'm good." Engels sat down, looking concerned about his surroundings. "Will this take long? I've been out of town, and I just want to get home and take a shower."

"Not too long. And I want to thank you for stopping by the police station on your way home."

"Your call made it sound important. And since I go right by here on my way home, it was an easy stop. So what's so important?"

"We just need some clarification from you about a situation that has come to our attention." Knight held up his hand. Then one finger at a time. "Fraud. Arson. And of course the pièce de résistance, murder."

Ralph jumped out of his chair. "What? I never killed nobody. Now if you'll excuse me, this conversation is over and I'm going home." He headed for the door.

"I'm sorry to be the bearer of bad news, but going home to shower is going to be impossible for you. Your home is a pile of burned rubble."

"Are you insane?" Ralph turned to face Knight and laid it

on real thick, hoping his acting skills would pass the smell test. "What are you talking about?"

"There was a fire at your house. It's a total loss. And your wife, Sally—I'm sorry to be the bearer of more bad news—is dead. The best we can figure is that someone slammed something heavy against her head and then set your house on fire."

Ralph's mouth fell open and he stumbled back into the chair, staring at Knight like he had three heads.

"I know what this is. A joke, right? Who put you up to this? Herbie? Conrad?"

"Not sure we know guys with those names. Care to give us last names too? We can check them out."

"I've been out of town. Making deliveries. You've got nothing on me or you would've read me my rights already."

"And those deliveries are where the fraud charge enters the picture. We have it on good authority that the pharmaceuticals you were delivering were not only stolen, but also out of date, and may have been tampered with, thereby making them contaminated as well."

"This can't be happening." He gazed around the room, staring into the two-way mirror, seeing only his own reflection. "My wife…Sally…"

"She was dead before the blast and thrown about thirty feet. The ME found blunt force trauma when he did the autopsy."

"An autopsy? You've already done an autopsy? When did all of this happen?"

"Yesterday. We had an incorrect phone number for you, and it took us a while to get it sorted out. Hence the urgency of our call today."

"This isn't real."

Someone opened the door and placed a bottle of water on the table in front of Ralph.

"Thanks." He twisted the cap and took a big gulp. "Sally. My poor Sally. How?… Who?"

"I've told you how, but I'm afraid we don't know who. That's where your help will be valuable. To help us catch the person who did this to Sally."

"I don't know anyone who would want to hurt Sally. She was a God-fearing, loving soul."

"Perhaps someone you disappointed in business. Selling outdated and contaminated pharmaceuticals can be a dangerous game. If you were to sell tainted insulin, for example, and a diabetic died as a result, someone's little girl perhaps. That person might hunt you down and seek revenge."

Ralph said nothing.

"But I gotta tell you, who we really want is the person pulling the strings. The top dog."

"That bitch?"

Moss, who was observing the interview, stepped closer to the glass. His internal radar sounded at the word. *Is Ralph just cursing or is a woman at the top? Soraya?*

Moss rang Knight's cell.

"Throw the name Soraya Rousseau at him. See what he does."

He could see Knight nod through the one-way glass.

"Does the name Soraya Rousseau mean anything to you?"

They all saw Ralph flinch.

"Liar. Got you," whispered Moss.

"Pretty name. Almost musical. But no, I can't say I know anyone with such a pretty name. And now that I think of it, I don't like where this interrogation is going. I'd like my lawyer here before we continue."

"Ralph. Ralphie. Your lawyer?" said Knight. "What's that going to do for you? I mean, it's your right and all. But this isn't an interrogation. Think of it as a friendly chat. The shock of finding out your house has been destroyed and your wife is dead has to be overwhelming. I know it would be for me."

"You got that right."

"Bring in a lawyer and it becomes a full-fledged interrogation, down to me reading you your Miranda rights. And then there's the paperwork. God knows how much I hate paperwork."

"I watch TV. I know how this works. Once I ask for a lawyer, you have to stop questioning me and let me make a phone call."

"You're right about that." Knight stepped back and leaned against the two-way mirror. "Lawyers are expensive. Two, three hundred dollars an hour. You have that kind of money?"

"Don't worry yourself about my finances, Detective."

"The other thing you really need to consider is who's paying for your lawyer? Are you paying for him, or is someone else footing the bill? And if someone else is paying the tab, where do you think the lawyer's loyalties will be?"

"Am I free to go? Or do I need to call my lawyer?"

"Yes, you're free to go, but don't you want to see your wife? The body? Say your goodbyes?"

"Oh, yeah, sure. Is she here?"

"We had her brought here for you. Didn't want you to have to drive all over town. Follow me."

They went down the hall to the elevators and then down to the basement. A small room had been designated as the morgue. Knight opened the door and waved Ralph inside. A young man in green scrubs who had been sitting on the lone chair in the closet-size room, his eyes glued to his iPad, snapped to attention. The only other piece of furniture was the gurney where a white sheet was draped over a body.

Ralph barely moved at first, and his hesitance and deep inhale surprised Knight.

"Whenever you're ready," said the technician.

"I guess I'm ready," said Ralph, who slowly approached the body.

Knight positioned himself next to Ralph as the technician drew back the sheet. Ralph winced when he saw the badly charred body of his wife. Identification was impossible since so little of what was Sally Engels remained.

"If it is any consolation, she was dead before the explosion," said Knight. "The ME found a large crack in her skull. Blunt force trauma. However it happened, whether from hitting her head after a fall, or being struck, she died instantly."

Ralph clutched a tissue to his eyes, blotting away tears. "She was a good soul, kind and loving. I don't know what I'm going to do without her."

You'll figure it out, you son of a bitch screamed the voice in Knight's head. "I'm sorry for your loss." He nodded to the technician, who drew the sheet up to cover Sally Engel's body.

Moss watched from the hall. *Crocodile tears. That's what they are*, he thought. Sally Engels hadn't been as innocent as she presented herself to be, but that didn't matter now. She was gone. Moss turned and left before Ralph saw him, wondering what Sally Engels had done to incur the wrath of others, to end her life so violently, fearing his visits might have signed her death warrant.

Ralph and Knight walked into the hall, "Can I go now?"

"Sure, but please stay in town. And let me just say, TV cop shows usually have better endings than the one I'm afraid you're facing here."

Howie pulled up to the 7-Eleven on Richmond Road at midnight, and a man dressed from head to toe in black jumped into the passenger seat of the U-Haul truck. Howie's shocked expression when he saw who his passenger was almost elicited a comment, but Moss pulled a gun and held it to Howie's mouth faster than flies on meat at a picnic.

"Shut up and drive," mouthed Moss, barely above a whisper.

Howie turned onto Monticello. "Do you know where we're going?"

"I'm the brawn. You're the brains. Go where they told you to go."

Howie took the bypass and made his way to Merrimac Trail and the remains of Ralph Engels' house. They could see the charred remains of the house when they pulled into the driveway, but the fire hadn't reached the back garage.

Engels was sitting in a lawn chair smoking a joint.

"About time you guys got here. We're on a tight schedule. Load everything."

Howie opened the back loading door on the truck. "Where's the rest of the crew?"

"You're it. Get to work."

"Ain't you gonna help?" Howie looked at Moss, who was leaning against the truck.

"I'm security. Can't do my job if I'm carrying boxes."

Two hours later the truck was full and the garage empty. Howie was sweating and panting from exertion.

"Guess you better lay off the Twinkies, fat boy," said Ralph, giving Howie's gut a poke.

"Shut the fuck up and get in the truck," said Howie.

"I'll be leading our little caravan in my own car. Stay close, but not too close. We're heading back through town and out Route Five to Chickahominy Park. There'll be more loading and unloading there, so rest up while you drive."

The vehicles pulled out.

"You could've helped, you know."

"Security doesn't do heavy lifting."

Howie followed Ralph down Monticello and out Route 5. There was no traffic so keeping Ralph in sight wasn't a problem.

From the parking lot of fire station five, Daniel watched two red dots approach Centerville Road. One GPS tracking beacon was glued to Moss's gun stock. If he was frisked, no one would think to check his gun for a tracker. The other tracker was attached to the bumper of Ralph's SUV.

"They're on their way. About five more miles and you should see them."

"Copy that," said Knight, who was secreted on the Charles City side of the bridge. Daniel had told him about Moss's request to let him handle the takedown alone, but Knight had men stationed in the area in case Moss needed some help. He knew even the best-laid plans usually went to shit as soon as the first move was made.

"This is a slick operation," said Jesse, who had begged his way into Daniel's car. He poured coffee out of the thermos for both of them.

"You're right," said Daniel. "Beautifully planned and synchronized."

"They rob warehouses in the dead of night, sit on the goods for a period of time, consolidate them at a distribution point to move them out of state, and funnel them into the legitimate supply chain, where unsuspecting customers buy them."

"Brilliant, really. Now to catch them in the act and shut it down."

"Think we'll manage that tonight?"

"Only time will tell." Daniel finished his coffee, wiped out the cup, and screwed it back onto the thermos.

"If there is a weak link, other than Howie, I put my money on Ralphie boy. Just gotta get him to sing like a bird."

"Wouldn't that be nice? But the good guys—that's us—don't usually get that lucky." The dots were right at the turnoff where Daniel was sitting. "Here they come."

"And there they go."

Daniel started his car but kept the headlights off, and pulled onto Monticello.

"I remember this place," said Howie, when Ralph made a right into the parking lot of Chickahominy Park and drove past the pool, then made another right down the dirt road toward the river.

"Where's he going? There's nothing back there but campsites and a boat ramp."

"You answered your own question. They must be moving the goods along the river."

"That makes no sense. You're very exposed on the river. Driving is faster, and no one can tell what's in the truck."

"Howie, it's not your job to ask questions. Just do as you're told and you might get out of this mess alive."

Ralph stopped at a campsite close to the boat ramp. A large RV was hooked up to power and two men came out to meet them. Moss recognized them as the same two men who cleared the cartons out of the storage shed Howie bought. The one wearing the Tupac T-shirt directed Howie as he backed the truck into a space alongside the RV.

"This here is Tupac, and the guy over there is Rip," said Ralph. "Get comfortable, 'cause we're spending the night. Tomorrow night starts the fun and games. Not too many people around this time of year, but don't go buddying up to anyone, or telling them our business. Bathrooms and showers are up that a way. I'll throw some blankets and a couple of pillows in the truck's cab for you."

"Why can't we sleep in the RV?"

"Hired help uses the outside facilities." Ralph slammed a flashlight into Howie's stomach. "Here, so you don't get lost. And watch out for bears."

"Bears? You're kidding, right?"

"This place is darker than a witch's ass," said Howie, while he and Moss walked back from the showers. "If I was planning an ambush, this would be the perfect place."

"That's comforting."

"Just trying to think like the bad guys."

"Don't think, Howie. No one's paying you to think."

When they got back to the truck Moss told Howie to take the back seat. "You're doing the heavy lifting. It'll be more comfortable for you to get some sleep back there."

"Ain't you the kind one?"

Moss smacked the back of his head. "Shut up and get in."

CHAPTER 27

"Rachel, I need to run something by you, and I want your honest opinion." Sara and Rachel were having an all-night Siamese mah jongg pajama party to keep from worrying about the men.

"I'm all yours. And our score is tied, so it's a good time to take a food and potty break. What's up?"

"It's about Moss. There was a moment when Moss and I—"

"Stop."

"What?"

"Please don't tell me about you and Moss."

"But you're my best friend. If I don't talk to you about him, who can I talk to?"

"I know, but I…he…you…"

"He's awesome."

"La-la-la-la-la" Rachel covered her ears.

"Come on, Rachel."

"Okay. Tell me. Go on. But no intimate details."

"Okay. Above the covers. He's awesome. Strong. Take charge. We had a moment…"

"Hope it lasted more than a moment."

Sara giggled. "Trust me, it was delightful, however long it lasted. And I guess that's what I want to talk to you about.

We kind of clicked. It was really good. The best I've had for…well, for a long time."

"That's a good thing."

"But is it? A thing? I mean could it…could we be a thing? Or is Moss what his name implies, a rolling stone that gathers no moss, no hangers on, no lasting relationships?"

"Interesting question, one I'm not sure I can answer."

"Damn. He's so…so…"

"I know."

"I can't get him out of my head, and I'd sure like him back in my bed again soon."

"Have you talked about anything more permanent?"

"No. And I don't want a full-time, live-in relationship. I like my freedom and my alone time."

"Then there's no reason why you can't have that and enjoy Moss when he comes to town. But you'll have to live with knowing you're sharing him with other women. Can you do that?"

"Good question."

Moss lay on his back in the front seat of the truck, staring at the ceiling of the truck cab. He'd run through his relaxation routine twice so far. Maybe the third rendition would work and he'd get some shut-eye. He could hear Howie snoring from the back seat and envied him. He really needed a few hours' sleep. There was work to be done, and he needed to be at the top of his game or people might get hurt.

His watch vibrated on his wrist. It was two AM. *Let the games begin.* With a predator's caution, Moss slipped out of the truck and into the RV. All was calm. Loud snoring greeted him. Ralph and his two goons were zonked.

Suddenly, the RV door slammed open behind him and Howie bounced into the RV. The three men jumped to their feet, guns drawn, while Moss hunkered down behind the door, out of sight.

"You ass," said Ralph. "What the fuck do you want?"

"It's cold out there," stomping into the sitting area. "Hired help or not, I'm bunking in here."

Howie turned to Moss for confirmation, but he was nowhere to be seen.

"Sure. Whatever," said Ralph. "Get some sleep. Tomorrow's a big day."

Ralph cooked breakfast. Bacon and eggs smelled great and the steaming hot coffee hit the spot on the chilly morning. They sat around the campfire and ate in silence.

"We'll spend most of today here and then set out tonight."

"Are we it?" asked Howie. "Is anyone else joining us?"

"You sure ask a lot of questions for hired help," said Ralph. The two other guys glowered at him. Moss kept his eyes on his plate.

"Don't mean anything by it. Just like to know the score."

"Shut up and finish your food. Then clean this mess up." Ralph put down his dish and rubbed his eyes.

"What's with the blinking? I swear your eyelids are flashing faster than a strobe light."

"More questions?" Ralph stared at Howie, then relented, deciding the kid meant no harm. "Allergies. I'm allergic to everything these days. Dust. Pollen. Peanut butter. You name it and my body has an issue with it. Being out here in the woods is deadly."

"My mom's got peanut allergies. Almost killed her about a week ago."

"Drives me crazy. Cold weather is the only thing that short-circuits it."

"Virginia doesn't qualify as cold. What brought you here?"

"Work, what else? Nosy SOB, aren't you?" Ralph looked at his watch and stood up. "I'm going up to Publix. Get some Benadryl. Then to a meeting. Be gone most of the day. You guys do some fishing. Play some poker. Whatever. Be ready to leave when the sun goes down."

Huge sunglasses covered much of her face as she waited in the Publix parking lot. An ankle-length black leather coat, knee-high black boots paired with a thigh-high black skirt and black turtleneck made her disappear into the black leather seats. The only visible color was the bright, killer-red lipstick Soraya applied using the visor mirror. She puckered and blew a kiss at her reflection.

Her cell rang.

"Yes?"

"Hello, my love. Just want to confirm our dinner plans at Upstairs?"

"My mouth is already watering. The best baked grouper I've ever had."

"What time do you think you'll arrive?"

"Make our reservations for eight. I'll be finishing up here tonight and my flight for Grand Cayman leaves tomorrow afternoon from Miami."

Ralph drove the five miles back to Williamsburg. When he pulled into the parking lot, he saw the fire-engine red Mercedes in the distance. He stopped at the edge of the Target lot and took stock of his situation. Her threatening words from their first meeting reverberated in his brain.

"Steal from me and I'll take your hand. Snitch on me and I'll cut out your tongue. Run from me and I'll cut off your feet. Betray me and I'll cut out your heart."

He felt a migraine coming on. The lights began to jump, tension knots slowly twisted into his temples. Cold sweats trickled down his back. He pulled at the collar of his shirt. Saliva secreted into his mouth, and a moment later he opened his car door, leaned over, and threw up breakfast.

"You okay?" asked a person walking by.

"Yeah. Must have been something I ate. I'm fine. Thanks."

He rinsed out his mouth with water and spit it on top of his vomit. Then he started his car and drove to his rendezvous.

Neither one of them got out of their car. Ralph rolled down his window, as did Soraya.

"What's the good word?"

"You go tonight. The boat will be there about eleven. The cartons that get loaded into the boat are marked, right?"

"As you instructed."

"Good. Split the rest between the RV and the truck. I don't want any slipups." Soraya did a quick scan of the parking lot, making sure no one was overly interested in their conversation. "Make sure you take care of the other business we discussed."

"I'm not sure I can do that."

"Really? Getting cold feet? Now? After all we've been through?"

"Killing puts a whole new slant on our operation."

"You killed Sally without blinking an eye."

"That was different." *Totally different,* thought Ralph, since he hadn't done the dirty deed, but paid Tupac to handle it. Better to let Soraya think he fulfilled the contract on poor Sally.

"How? She was your friggin' wife."

"In name only. Hired help."

"You are a cold-blooded, heartless bastard, aren't you?"

"Takes one to know one."

Soraya smiled. "Perhaps you're not properly motivated. I'm told a motivated person can move mountains."

"It's the other guy. Moss? He gives me the willies."

"I've known him to do that."

"Who is he? What does Moss do?"

"He's a fixer."

"A fixer? What does that mean?"

"He fixes things. Someone has a problem, alerts Moss, and he resolves it."

"Amicably?"

"Not always. But he definitely gets the job done." Soraya picked at her cuticle for a moment. "Don't worry about Moss. He knows what he's doing. Just make sure your guys follow through. And you finish your job at the end."

Ralph returned at dusk with buckets of KFC and containers of mashed potatoes, green beans, a tub of gravy, biscuits, and a case of Bud.

"Eat up. You'll need your strength. We go tonight. The boat arrives around eleven."

The five men gobbled up the food like it was their last meal.

"Just as its name implies, finger-lickin' good," said Howie, hoping to ease the tension. But no one laughed. "Have you guys done this before?"

"Again with the questions," said Ralph. "Done what? Ate chicken?"

"No. What we're doing tonight."

"And what exactly is that?" asked one of Ralph's cohorts.

Howie stared at him. "That's the thing. I don't know what that is. I picked up this dude, drove to a burned-out mess of what was once a house, loaded some boxes, drove the truck here, and spent the night. What exactly are we doing tonight?"

"More of the same," said Ralph. "You're driving the truck to North Carolina."

"North Carolina? I thought I was driving to Lenexa."

"Change of plans. Got a problem with that?"

"Guess not."

"It's a simple job, Howie. And for that you're being paid handsomely."

"Got to admit, the money's damn good. I don't think I want to know what's in the boxes."

"Ignorance is bliss," said Tupac. "If I were you, I'd stick with that."

Moss heard the faint sound of a motor approaching the boat landing. "We've got company."

Ralph and his two goons headed down to the narrow dock. Howie and Moss stood back.

"Remember, Howie. Just do as you're told. Don't think. Don't improvise. Follow orders."

They watched Ralph and Tupac catch the two lines thrown to them and tie up the boat.

"I know the guy in the boat. His name is Bob Smith."

"Bob Smith? Really? Could just as well be John Doe."

"He brought me into this. Gave me the money to buy the storage shed."

"It's a tight-knit group. They don't like outsiders. Or loose ends, so stay sharp."

"What's that supposed to mean?"

Moss shot Howie a look that had the intended effect.

Howie ducked his chin and ground his foot into the dirt like a recalcitrant child. "Now's not the time to get stupid. You know exactly what that means."

Ralph came up to them. "Howie, open the truck and take out the boxes addressed to Dr. Watson. Get them to the boat. My guys will help this time. Then you and Moss get in the truck. Here's where you're going." He handed Howie a slip of paper with a Raleigh, North Carolina address. "Should take you about three hours. Take Route 85. Will take you a little longer, but you won't get the itch to speed."

"Gotcha."

"Call this number when you arrive and they'll tell you where to go."

Howie opened the back of the U-Haul and climbed in. The other two guys stayed on the ground and took the boxes Howie handed them down to the boat. Moss also stayed on the ground, but got real curious when he realized the load of cartons was significantly smaller than what they took from the garage the previous night. Many of the boxes had been removed, but he hadn't seen it happen. *Where'd they go?*

Moss sidled up to Ralph, out of earshot of the others. "Don't mean to tell you your business, but you've been robbed."

"How you figure?"

Moss pointed to Howie and his men relocating the boxes. "There aren't half the number of boxes there now. Where'd the rest go?"

A malevolent smile crossed Ralph's face. "Observant, aren't you?"

"It's what I get paid for. Only I didn't see it happen."

"Don't get your boxers in a bunch. That's what showers are for. My guys moved a few into the RV while you were cleaning up."

"Not sure you-know-who will be pleased with their disappearance."

"Not to worry. I'm following orders. They're just going to a different destination."

Moss stroked his chin as he walked away. Three loads of boxes, one in the RV, one in the boat, and what's left in the truck, each going someplace different. He knew he couldn't cover all three. Time to call in reinforcements without alerting Ralph.

As Moss pulled out his cell, a hand shot out, attempting to grab his arm. Moss caught Tupac's arm by the wrist in mid-swing and twisted it around in one graceful motion that took Tupac down to the ground. He went down hard, legs splayed, his head hitting a tree root. Moss's boot landed barely an inch from his jewels.

"Move and I'll put you out of commission for the rest of your life."

Tupac raised his hands off the dirt, surrendering.

"You don't ever want to touch me. Capish?"

"Hey, man. What ya gotta go and do that for? No need to get crazy."

Howie watch in awe. He sensed a rising tension between Moss and Tupac, like two rams ready to lock horns.

CHAPTER 28

"What's going on here?" demanded Ralph as he rushed to Tupac's aid.

"He was making a call. You said no phones."

"You never told me that," said Moss. "And I gotta call my woman and let her know I'll be gone another night."

"She got you on a tight leash?" asked Ralph. "You don't look the type."

"Just being respectful, is all. You can listen if you want."

"This is Sara. I'm not able to take your call. Please leave a message and I'll call you back." He left a message and ended the call. "There. Nothing to it."

Tupac had remained on the ground the entire time, and Moss held out his hand to help him up. "No hard feelings, right?"

"Nah. Just following orders. Ralph said no calls. Figured that went for all of us. Didn't know you were special."

"Now you know."

Moss's call to Sara went unanswered but reached its intended target—Daniel. The cryptic message only gave hints about the current situation, but it was enough for him to relay to Knight, who had eyes and ears monitoring the campgrounds.

"Makes sense," said Knight. "They've loaded a boat. Along with the truck that makes two modes of transport. Since Moss used the number three, I'm guessing there are cartons in the RV."

"Wouldn't it be easier to take them down at the campgrounds rather than let them head out?" asked Jesse.

"That's the plan, but we need a little more time to get our guys in position," said Knight.

"Be great if Moss can stall their departure, but he'd have to be a mind reader to know we're not ready yet," said Jesse.

"He's done stranger things, so don't count it out just yet," said Daniel.

"I gotta drop a load," said Howie.

"Use the bushes," said Ralph, pointing to the trees, "so you don't have to go up to the bathrooms. We're getting ready to leave and I want us all pulling out together."

"I am not taking a crap in the bushes. You can wait five minutes." Howie turned and broke into a trot as he headed to the bathroom.

"Make it fast," yelled Ralph.

Moss smiled while he watched him go. He knew the few precious minutes Howie was stealing from everyone leaving were vital minutes that could mean the difference between success and failure. He prayed his message reached the intended ears and was understood.

Movement to his left caught Moss's attention, the vague shape of someone crouching low to the ground. Footfalls to his right. Someone was climbing the river bank. He warbled a two-note alert. Daniel responded.

"When he gets back, we're outta here," said Ralph. "Tupac, you and Rip unhook the electrical and get the RV ready to move. Bob, you head back to the boat."

Howie came walking down the path like a man without a care in the world. His expression changed when he saw Rip and Ralph waiting for him at the bottom of the hill.

"Took you long enough," said Rip.

"You can't rush these things. If I'm gonna be bouncing around in a truck for three hours, I gotta take care of business. Know what I mean?"

"Saddle up," said Ralph. "Let's go."

Rip used two flashlights to give Howie signals to get him on the path toward the road.

"Slow down to a crawl when you make the turn at the pool," said Moss. "I'm going to open the door and jump out."

"What? Why?"

"Just do it. When you get to the road, make the right and head on your way."

With a little effort Moss ducked out of the truck's cab. His left arm rolled over the sharp edge of a large rock and he grunted as a residual pain from his now-healed gunshot wound shot through him. He flexed his fingers and unsnapped his holster, removed his SIG Sauer P365, and held it low, pressed against his thigh. Its weight felt good in his hand.

As he headed back toward the campsite he could see the RV hadn't moved. In the dim light he saw Tupac and Rip up front, but there was no sign of Ralph. The boat was still tied to the dock, but there was no sign of Bob, the guy from the boat. Movement in the shadows caught his eye just as the

RV's engine roared to life and Ralph emerged from the trees, fiddling with his zipper. He gave Tupac a hand signal and walked down to the dock.

In less than a New York minute Ralph found himself faceup on the ground, his arm twisted in an unnatural position, a stiletto black leather boot thrust under his chin, restricting his breathing to hurried gasps.

"Where did you come from?"

"I'm everywhere." Daggers shot from her eyes, but her smirk had an "I dare you to try it" quality to it. *Shit,* thought Ralph *this is one dangerous woman. Lethal.*

"Help me up. We can get out of here by boat." He pointed down the dock where the motor boat was still tied up.

"A boat ride. How pleasant." Soraya followed Ralph down to the dock.

"Where's Mr. Smith?"

"He's taking care of our friends. You know how much he enjoys his work."

Ralph bent down to untie the boat from its cleat while Soraya leaned over him.

The garrote found home, looped with lightning speed over Ralph's head, as her boot pushed into Ralph's back for extra leverage, slicing smoothly through his flesh, cutting larynx and jugular with one easy motion. It was over almost before it began. Ralph's hands reached for his throat and were quickly soaked with his own blood. His final words gurgled, his eyes popped in terror. And then it was over…for him anyway…as he landed in a heap of human flesh on the dock.

Soraya stepped over him, untied the lines from the cleat and got in the boat. She started the engine, backed up to clear the dock, turned the wheel, and headed out into the night.

Moss warbled and heard the return cry. He followed the sound and caught up with Daniel outside the RV.

"I'm surprised they haven't pulled out yet," said Moss. "Ralph wanted everyone to leave at the same time. Wonder what they're waiting for."

"I heard a boat motor, so that's gone."

"Shit. That means someone got away."

"Not necessarily. Knight said he had a few boats patrolling the river. We could get lucky."

Moss gave him a cockeyed stare. "In your experience, how often do the good guys get lucky?"

"Rarely, I'll give you that. But it could happen."

"Ready to hit the RV?"

"It's showtime."

The two men stealthily approached the RV's door, staying clear of the front windshield.

"I only see Tupac behind the wheel," said Moss. "Stay alert. Rip's around somewhere."

Moss's powerful boot slammed open the door. They ducked and covered their ears as Daniel hurled a flash grenade into the RV. The loud blast and light stunned Tupac and he fumbled his way outside. Moss tackled Tupac, dropped him to the ground, rolled him onto his stomach and applied flex cuffs before he knew what hit him.

"Where's Ralph?" asked Moss.

"Who the fuck *are* you?" asked a stunned Tupac.

"I'm asking the questions. Where's Ralph?"

"Don't know."

Daniel moved cautiously into the back of the RV, his drawn Glock leading the way. A touch at his shoulder told him Moss had his back. Labored breathing revealed a hiding place. Daniel held up a fist motioning Moss to stop. Hand signals telegraphed enough information to get them on the same page. Moss moved stealthily to the other side of the door. One finger. Then two. Then three. Moss crashed his foot into the door, smashing it inward, splinters of fiberglass pummeling the man cowering in the darkness.

"Who do we have here? Daniel meet Rip," said Moss.

The muscle-bound man, sweating profusely, struggling to breathe, huddled in the dark. Thick neck, short arms, deep-set, almost black, eyes, greasy black hair, and a face full of stubble surrounding full lips and nicotine-stained teeth.

"Get up."

"Asthma." He coughed. "Can't breathe. Inhaler." He pointed to a duffel bag lying on the bed.

"Slow. Move slow."

Barely able to stand erect, Rip unzipped the bag, pulled the inhaler out, took two hits, and straightened up, opening his mouth wide and sucking in a gulp of air.

"Better?"

"Yeah. Thanks."

"Come on. Let's join your friend," said Daniel as he secured Rip's hands behind his back with flex cuffs.

Howie never left the parking lot. He pulled the truck to the side of the road, jumped out, and raced back to the RV. He saw a flash of light and heard the explosion inside the RV which stopped him in his tracks.

He heard a twig snap, turned around and got cold-cocked. Then his assailant's hands were around his neck.

"Bob? Bob Smith?" he gasped, pushing against the assailant's chest. "Stop. It's me. Howie. What are you doing? I'm on your side."

"Like hell you are."

Bob applied more pressure and squeezed tighter. Howie's arms flailed as he attempted to knock the two hundred-plus behemoth off his chest. Howie got his leg free and slammed his knee into Bob's groin. Bob screamed in pain and fell backwards, giving Howie time to get to his feet.

Howie spit out a bloody glob of tooth, cheek and tongue, wishing he had water to rinse away the metallic taste of the blood. When he looked up, Bob was pointing a gun at him.

"What's wrong with you?" asked Howie, choking and gasping for breath.

"Nothing. Cleaning up a loose end is all." He pulled the trigger.

CHAPTER 29

Daniel almost tripped over an unconscious Howie lying facedown in the dirt. *Shit.*

"Aggggggggh," moaned Howie when Daniel bent down to check his pulse. He could see blood pooling under his thigh.

"Lie still, Howie, you've been shot." Into his mic Daniel said, "Man down. Need EMS and an ambulance."

"What happened?" asked Moss, rushing to his side.

"The kid took a bullet."

"Damn, man. Sara's gonna be pissed."

"EMS is on the way, Howie." Daniel pulled off Howie's belt and used it for a tourniquet. "That should do until EMS gets here. Don't move."

"He's pale as a ghost and sweating like a pig," said Jesse, who'd stayed on the sidelines like he was told, but joined the group when he heard the gunshot.

"The guy ran into the woods when Howie went down," said Jesse. He pulled a water bottle out of his backpack, knelt down, and cradled Howie's head while he touched the bottle to his lips. "He better not die. Sara's going to go nuts if he does. She'll never forgive herself."

"No one's going to die. Cut the kid some slack. He's new at this undercover stuff," said Moss. "He'll do fine."

EMS arrived and started treatment, then loaded Howie into the ambulance and sped off.

"You never really know what someone is capable of until the opportunity presents itself," said Jesse, watching the ambulance leave.

"Let's find Knight and see what's left to be done."

They caught up with Knight at the foot of the dock standing over a body.

"Looks like Ralphie met his maker."

Moss bent down. "A garrote? Yikes. Rough way to go."

"Any guesses as to whose handiwork this might be?"

"Yep. A signature move of someone I know only too well." Moss shook his head.

Rotors turning overhead caught their attention. A black helicopter approached and hovered over the bridge.

"One of yours?" asked Daniel.

"Yes," said Knight. "Reinforcements. Just in case."

"Tell them to head upriver. The boat's gone, so I'm guessing she left by water."

"She?" asked Daniel.

"Soraya," said Moss. "Using a garrote has her fingerprints all over it. More exotic than a gun or knife."

"It's a wide river. Not sure our search will produce results," said Knight.

"One can hope," said Moss.

They'd all started back to their cars when Daniel's attention was drawn by movement to his left.

"We've got a rabbit," yelled Daniel, who heard rustling in the bushes and saw a guy dash out across the field.

"I'm on him," said Knight. He quickly lowered his night-vision goggles since the running guy was all in black, which made him hard to see.

Thank God, thought Daniel. *I'm too old for this chasing shit.* Once, a long time ago, that would have been him giving chase, but now he knew and accepted his limitations. He envied Knight's full speed sprint across the field, watching him disappear through the trees in hot pursuit.

"Who do you think that is?" asked Jesse.

"The only person not accounted for is the guy who shot Howie," said Daniel.

Within minutes Knight was back, leading a flex-cuffed suspect by the scruff of the neck.

"Meet Mr. Smith, if that's his real name," said Knight. He beckoned to two of his men and they escorted Smith to a waiting police car.

Soraya saw the helicopter's light beam approaching from the south. She maneuvered the small boat along the shoreline and cut the engine when the helicopter got close. Better to hide in the shadows for a time.

Nothing had gone according to plan, and she'd have some explaining to do, but she could sell sand to a desert sheik. She relentlessly pushed herself, seeing only the life she wanted, willing to do whatever was necessary to accomplish her goals. Making sure her life was perfect—undisturbed, unaffected. People were unimportant specimens of human fodder, designed to fail and disappoint, and who ended up just getting in the way. Use them for what minimum service or entertainment they might provide, exploit them when possible, then toss them aside like the day's trash.

But then there was Moss. Someone she bedded. Someone she had planned to partner with. *Oh, Moss. What can I say? It's better to go out in a blaze of glory than slink out the back door with barely a whimper.* The best-laid plans seldom prospered, and Moss was now a thorn in her side who needed to be plucked and ground to dust. She added his demise to her mental to-do list.

When the helicopter was out of sight, she continued her journey upriver and pulled in at the Rockahock campgrounds. She tied up the boat loosely, retrieved the extra gas can, and spilled some gasoline onto a rag. Igniting it, she tossed it into the boat and watched the flames catch. Then she untied the lines and pushed the boat away from shore.

Her deep exhale when she got into her car blew away the failure of the evening's activities. She had a dinner date tonight at one of her favorite restaurants on Grand Cayman Island and she planned on keeping it. She pulled out of the campgrounds, navigating the dark local road until she got onto Route 30, tuned in Wagner's *Ride of the Valkyries*, and sped off into the night.

Knight's phone rang as he, Daniel, Jesse, and Moss stood talking at their cars.

"When?"

One-sided conversations were hard to decipher, but they all could tell something was wrong.

"Damn."

"What happened?" asked Daniel.

"He's dead, isn't he?" said Moss. "The guy you tackled on the field, our rabbit, didn't make it to the police station."

"Are you prescient, Moss?" asked Knight.

"No. But it makes sense. The dead can't talk. Can't ask for immunity."

"How?" asked Jesse. "He was in police custody."

"Don't have all the details, but it sounds like he fell on his sword."

"Suicide?" Jesse was incredulous.

"Better than waiting to get stuck with a shiv in jail. These are high-stakes games. Winner takes all. Losers lose all."

"Who's left alive?" asked Daniel. "Who have we got that can help put the pieces of this puzzle together?"

"Tupac and Rip," said Knight. "Low-lying fruit. I don't imagine they know much beyond their own jobs."

"You may want to make some extra security arrangements for them," said Daniel. "What about Soraya?"

"Yes. Soraya." Moss muttered and turned towards the river.

"I'm assuming she got away in the boat," said Knight. "I can put a BOLO out for her. Do you know what she's driving?"

"A red Mercedes. My guess is she'll dump it for something less flashy."

"Driving seems too conspicuous to me," said Daniel. "She'd have to know we'd put out an alert."

"We can also check the local airports if you think it would help." Knight pulled out his cell, ready to make the call.

"Knowing Soraya, she's long gone. Evaporated into the night," said Moss. "The best you can do is get a list of any private flights out of Williamsburg airport, or any other private landing strips, in the next twenty-four hours. Maybe we can get a flight plan, but those are easy to change once airborne."

"She has to land somewhere," said Jesse.

"True, but it won't be on American soil. And without a tail number there's no way to trace it."

"Worth a try," said Knight. "I'll get on it."

"So…it's over? At least in our little corner of the world?" asked Jesse.

"This is nowhere near over," said Moss. "Soraya may be in the wind, but I know she's up to her pretty eyeballs in this."

"Do you think you'll ever catch her?" asked Daniel.

"Who knows? Soraya is smart and very resourceful. If

234

she resurfaces and indulges in her old tricks, we might have a chance. But the woman knows how to disappear."

"If I were her, I'd plant myself on some tropical island and wallow in my ill-gotten gains," said Jesse.

"Guess you won't be going back to chasing drug traffickers in Wachapreague. Sounds like your services may be needed elsewhere."

"You got that right, Daniel," laughed Moss. "This is better. Chasing Soraya is going to be way more fun than cleaning fish."

Howie saw a blur of shadows when he opened his eyes. "What happened? Where am I?"

"You got shot. That's what happened," said Daniel. "You're in the hospital."

Another face appeared in the haze. "Didn't anyone ever tell you you're supposed to dodge bullets, not stop them?" asked Moss.

"Huh? Shot?"

"Don't you remember?"

"N...no." Howie closed his eyes for a few moments. "Burning...my leg..." He propped himself up and looked at his bandaged leg.

"Take it easy, there," said someone in scrubs when sirens started to howl. "No fast movements." The nurse adjusted the monitors and turned to Howie. "You've had surgery. The doctors repaired the damage." She put a hand on Howie's shoulder. "You're going to be fine, and the doctor should be in shortly to speak with you."

Haltingly, Howie's eyes moved down from his chest to his waist to his legs. Wrinkling his nose in concentration, he tried to wiggle his toes. Only one foot's toes moved.

"My leg! I can't feel my leg. Or move my toes."

"You're not paralyzed," said the nurse. "Just very sore."

"Don't worry," said Daniel. "The doc said the bullet didn't hit anything major. A through-and-through. Regular bullet, not a hollow point. You're going to be fine. You'll be sore, need some PT to build back muscle strength, and probably need a cane, but hey, some women find that sexy."

"Welcome to the club," added Moss.

"What club?" mumbled Howie.

"The I-got-shot-and-survived club."

"Did you get 'em?"

"*We* got 'em." Daniel emphasized the *we*. "None of this would have been possible without you, Howie. You're sort of a hero."

"Whatever you do, don't tell my mom."

"Too late for that, son." Sara leaned over the bed and kissed his forehead.

"Guess I kind of screwed up…again."

"Nonsense. As Daniel said, you're a hero."

It had been a brutal twenty-four hours of worry, and Sara felt relief wash through her when she heard the car door slam and watched Moss come up the walk. She had the door open before he could ring the bell and fell into his arms.

"You okay?" Moss held her tightly.

"Not even close. But I know Howie's in good hands."

"What can I do?"

"I think we're about to do it."

Moss brushed his thumb lightly over Sara's lips, his eyes meeting hers, seeing in them a longing he didn't expect. Sara's lips parted when her eyes met his.

"I know the romantic thing to do is to scoop you into my

arms and carry you into the bedroom, but I'm afraid my scooping days are behind me."

Sara took his hand and led him down the hall. "Walking works."

She felt him behind her, then his warmth against her. Comforting. She turned to him at the foot of the bed. His fingertips traced the line of her chin, stopping at her lips. He moved closer, his heat escalating, his eyes drinking her in.

She paused for a moment. "Viagra?"

"I admit to being a little tired after last night, but it's not necessary, thank you for asking. I'll do my part without chemical assistance."

"Good to know."

Burning lips danced across her skin, tugged at her nipples and again found her lips, demanding more, deeper kisses. Her head was spinning, her hands moving up and down his back, pulsing muscles bursting with heat. Her fingers groped for his shirt buttons. He pushed them away and ripped his shirt open.

Sara giggled. "Are you trying out for a sex video?"

"No, just didn't want you wasting your efforts. Besides, it's an old shirt and I've always wanted to do that."

"Never deny yourself what you've always wanted to do."

She pushed his shirt off his shoulders, stroking his chest and running her hands up his back. Her thumbs followed his collarbone to his Adam's apple, leaning in and tickling it with her tongue. His erection swelled.

"I think it's my turn to catch you up." He undid three ivory buttons and pulled the powder blue ribbon keeping her blouse closed at her cleavage. The fabric fell away, revealing a lacy blue bra.

"You match!"

"Always," she purred.

His hands slid down her hips, taking her pants with them.

Daintily, she stepped out of her pants and panties, and slid under the covers, holding them up for him, watching him wiggle out of his jeans. Warm skin against warm skin. He rolled himself on top of her. The scent of him toyed and teased her senses.

"Any preferences I need to be aware of?"

"Ah, a considerate lover."

"I aim to please."

"Surprise me."

"With pleasure."

His hands went into motion, roaming her body with abandon. Lips covered her with kisses. Starting at her neck, he nibbled her, his fingertips making their way between her breasts, lingering to play with her nipples, then continuing downward, finding that sweet spot…nirvana! She cooed in his ear, her hips rising, twisting, gyrating, intensifying the depth of his touch. His lips crushed hers, his kiss demanding, his tongue searching her, reaching out for her, finding her.

"You are beautiful." The moon shone through the transom, illuminating her face. "In the moonlight, you look like a porcelain doll."

"Have no fear. I won't break."

She moved from beneath him, mounting him.

"My turn on top," she whispered into his ear, her tongue flicking in and out, licking his ear's rim, her hands finding gold.

"You are enjoying me."

"Yes, every strapping, hunky, sexy inch of you."

His hands embraced her head and pulled her close, kissing her hard, stealing her breath.

Then his fingers found her special place, and a lightning bolt shot through her. Her gasp urged him onward. Faster, deeper. Deeper, faster. She was so wet, so ready for him. And he was so ready for her. He burned to enter her.

Gentle fingers encircled his manhood, stroking, pumping, massaging, guiding him as he entered her. Wave upon wave of energy fueled their lovemaking. Sara gasped and murmured. Moss's guttural moans reverberated through the room.

Their repeated lovemaking left them both panting and exhausted by dawn. When Sara finally opened her eyes she saw Moss enter the bedroom with a tray with coffee and croissants.

"Breakfast is ready, m'lady."

"Thank you. I can't remember the last time someone served me breakfast in bed." She added cream to her coffee. "Oh, now I remember. Never."

"I like being first at something with you."

"You've been first at something more important than breakfast."

"Do you know you do the cutest thing with your nose when you're making a point?"

"Seriously? My nose?"

"Yes. You sort of wrinkle it up, every time you laugh, and sort of down when you're confused. Can't really explain it, but it is cute."

"I know Rachel does that thing with her eyebrow when she wants to make a point, but a lot of people can do that. Never gave my nose a thought."

"Then your nose wrinkle is unique...like you."

"Why didn't you ever settle down? Do the family thing?"

"Relationships are hard. They move. They get better. They get worse. Good times. Hard times. Bad times. Relational stasis doesn't exist. I'm just not good at them."

"Considering my two failed marriages, and all Howie's problems, I agree. They are hard."

"I didn't want to be responsible for someone else. I know it sounds selfish, but I was a real screwup when I was young. Kind of like Howie. Disappointed a lot of people."

"We're all screwups when we're young." Sara finished her croissant, licking a dollop of jelly off her finger.

"Well, I was big time, not small potatoes. I had trouble taking care of me. Figured I wouldn't be very good at taking care of someone else. The military straightened me out, but when I got home I fell into the same shit. It took a long time to work my way out."

"And now?"

"Now, I'm on a different path. Think my hero gene has taken charge of my body." He reached out and stroked her face. "But it's a lonely path, one that doesn't leave room for family or committed relationships."

Moss's cell interrupted. He listened intently, then ended the call.

"What was that about?"

"New assignment."

"Already?"

"No rest for the weary."

"I understand. And it's fine. I'll be here when you want to park your shoes under my bed. No strings attached."

CHAPTER 30

After few days' rest, everyone gathered at Rachel's for a hero's barbecue.

"I know this sounds crazy, but thanks," said Howie when he and Moss were enjoying beers on the finished new dock down by the river. "I couldn't have done it without you."

"I'm sorry it didn't work out better for you. Getting shot isn't fun."

"Don't I know it. Really, Moss. I know it wasn't my choice. You forced me all the way. But you stayed with me and I owe you big time. Even when I went down, you didn't run. Shit, I would have hightailed it out of there faster than shit through a duck if our positions were reversed. I'm not cut out for this G.I. Joe shit. Know what I mean?"

"I do, but you're wrong. I was watching you. Now I just have to teach you how to move...you know, duck and weave." Moss moved his arms from side to side. "Oh, and how to shoot. And it will be my honor to do that when you're ready."

"Why?"

"Why what?"

"Why are you going to do anything for me? I screwed up. Almost got us all killed."

"And you're the one who got shot. Big price to pay. You're going to have a limp."

"Yeah, but I hear it will help me with women."

"You'll certainly have a great story to tell them."

"About that story…how does it end? For me, I mean. I'm tired of being the loser, college dropout, job-hopper, especially in my mother's eyes."

"I hear you." Moss shook his head. "And your mom doesn't share your sentiment. She's just worried about you. Funny, my mom used to worry about me. I was trouble when I was your age."

"You?"

"Yeah. On the outside I was Mr. Cool, but inside I was running as fast as I could to keep showing up like the guy others saw as cool."

"Like a duck."

"Huh?"

"Old joke. On the surface of the pond, ducks swim gracefully, but under the water their little feet are paddling like crazy."

"Profound, Howie. Very profound."

"What straightened you out?"

"Marines."

"Don't think I'm cut out for the military, and my mom would have a shit fit if I joined up."

They fell into silence, each lost in his own thoughts.

"I need to find my own way," said Howie, finishing his beer. "It's tough. I'm used to running away when it gets tough. Not this time. I'm done running. I'm sticking."

"Sounds like you've finally make a good choice for yourself."

"What charges am I facing?"

"I don't do charges. You'll have to talk to Detective Knight or the feds about that."

"What's your best guess?"

"If you're lucky and get yourself a great lawyer, you could get probation. Maybe some community service."

"And if my lawyer sucks?"

"Seven to ten for possession, selling drugs, and fencing stolen goods."

"Guess I better get a good lawyer. Know any?"

"Nope. Lawyers wear suits and I'm a jeans guy. But when you find one, I'll pay the tab."

"Morgan? Morgan, where are you?"

"My office, where else?" She rolled her shoulders back and forth a few times, twisted her neck and pulled each arm up and over her head.

His face was flushed when she turned around to look at him. "What's got you so hot and bothered?"

"I got a call. The Herald's editorial board approved the story we're working on. They're offering us big money, and they want to run an excerpt."

"You're kidding!"

"Nope. Said they'd give it a front-page spot. Three columns wide. The editor is flying down here tomorrow to meet with us about the piece."

"That's odd."

"Not really." Jesse's excitement was over the top. "The guy said he wants to debrief us so he can get an opinion piece about skyrocketing drug costs ready to run on the same day."

"Who's writing that?"

"He didn't say, but the Herald has great writers, so I'm sure it'll be someone who can put the proper spin on the contaminated medications issue and get the fingers pointing in the right direction."

"Toward big pharma?"

"You got it."

"Jesse, there's a question I've been meaning to ask you."

"Oh? What's that?"

"The vials. What happened to the two vials of drugs that you brought back from the Congo? You never mentioned them after you got back from seeing Ravi."

"I gave them back."

"That's why they let me go."

"They were empty, and I had the results I needed from Ravi's tests. I didn't need to hold onto to the physical vials. He'd be a witness to their existence if proof was ever required. And I have photographs of them and a notarized statement that they existed."

"So I guess we don't have to sit on our story. It can be published," said Morgan.

"Can you imagine the outcry when the public finds out that some of the medications they rely on to keep them healthy could be substandard, tainted, or might even be killing them?" Jesse opened the mini fridge. "I need a beer."

"That has to be a secret worth keeping to whomever is behind any counterfeiting scheme," said Morgan.

"You've got that right. Prosecuting people caught buying, adulterating, and then reselling the most commonly used pharmaceuticals has to be kept off the front page."

"Not that anyone reads newspapers anymore."

"A lot of seniors do. But it doesn't matter. Their meds, treating conditions like high cholesterol, heart issues, and diabetes, are often targets of tampering because when they don't get better, it will be attributed to age, or their disease advancing, and they'll be prescribed a higher dose, or they'll die and any evidence of a substandard drug disappears with the body. And if they do complain, old people are easy to brush off and ignore."

"This is going to be so much fun," said Morgan.

"Fun?"

"Yes. It's a political hot potato. People are clamoring for less expensive drugs and the politicians promise to deliver. The bastards lie. They care more about retaining their power and their fancy perks than serving the people they supposedly represent. They'll lie, spin, kiss babies, say whatever needs to be said, steal—do anything and everything to make themselves look good."

A buzzing timer brought them both to the kitchen, where Jesse slid a tray of cocktail franks out of the oven.

"What are you doing? We're going to Rachel's for a barbecue."

"Consider these an appetizer. I'm hungry." He squeezed mustard on one of the franks and bit into it. "I detest politicians. If their lips are moving, they're lying. They go into Congress as regular people wanting to do good, get bought by the dark side, and leave as billionaires. They've got gold-plated health plans and can afford to buy branded drugs, not generics, so they're getting the full medication and not something that's biosimilar."

"As I said," Morgan smiled, "this is going to be fun. The outcry, politicians trying desperately to cover their asses. The only thing that will be better is watching big pharma try to cover their asses. They may have friends in high places, but those friends are going to jump ship fast if and when more bad stuff gets into the mainstream drug supply chain. And mark my words, that is definitely going to happen. We're going to have some mighty sick people dropping like flies at an Orkin picnic."

"Nice phrasing. Maybe we can use it in our story."

"Maybe. Go change your clothes. We're late for Rachel's."

Jesse picked up the remote to shut off the TV but froze.

Morgan sucked in a breath at the breaking news crawl. She hit the sound button.

"We've just learned that a private flight from Williamsburg to Miami disappeared a few days ago over the Okefenokee Swamp. The chartered plane was registered to the World Health Organization and was said to be carrying three passengers in addition to the pilot and one crew member. A search has been launched for the wreckage but it is being hampered by a severe weather front stalled over the area. We'll bring you more details as they become available."

"Wow," said Morgan. "A WHO plane? You don't think?"

"I don't know what to think. But the timing fits. Moss told me he followed Soraya to the airport a few days ago, before the shit hit the fan at the campgrounds, and watched while boxes were loaded and the plane took off. He thinks Soraya left by plane, and I know Matamba had already left when I checked the Williamsburg Inn."

"Too much of a coincidence?"

"There's no such thing as coincidence. Can't wait to see what Daniel and Knight say about it."

"Hey, Lette. How are you today?" asked Debra McKenna, sitting down at the table where Lette was drawing a picture. "That's a nice picture. Who are those people?"

"Just some people." Lette shrugged. "This is me." She pointed to a little girl. "And the dog's name is Tucker."

"That's a wonderful name for a dog. Do you know what type of dog he is?"

"He's a yellow lab. And he follows me around wherever I go. Or he used to." She swallowed, and her shoulders drooped a little.

"Used to? Did something happen to Tucker?"

"N-No… I don't know…" Lette picked up a green crayon and started coloring in grass.

"I've got some people I want you to meet, Lette. They're very nice, and they came a long way to meet you. Would you like to meet them?"

"I suppose so."

Debra stood up and held out her hand. Lette put down the crayon, stood, and took Debra's hand. Together they walked into the hall. "Hi, Detective Knight. Are you here to meet the nice people too?"

"I'm here to see you, Lette. How are you doing?"

"I'm good. Dr. Debra has some people she wants me to meet. Can you come too?" Lette grabbed onto his hand.

"If you want me to, I'd love to come with you."

"Good." Her grip tightened.

The three of them walked down the hall together, got in the elevator and went down to the first floor education and learning center.

"Lette, if you feel uncomfortable in any way, I want you to let me know and we can leave. Do you understand?"

"Yes, ma'am."

Debra opened the door to classroom one, and Tucker opened the door to Lette's heart. The dog was on her in a flash, licking and twisting and turning, his tail was going a mile a minute. Then Lette saw the man and woman, seated quietly on the sofa. Tears streamed down her cheeks as she walked slowly to them.

"Do you know who we are?" asked the woman.

"Do you remember us?" asked the man.

"Mommy! Daddy!" And then Lette was in her mother's arms, in their arms. "She told me you were dead."

"We're not. We never stopped looking for you. And Tucker is the happiest I've seen him since you disappeared."

Debra reached out for Adam's hand. "We did good," she whispered.

"From your lips to God's ears. You are so right."

Lette looked back at Debra and Detective Knight. "These are my friends."

"I know. We've met. They helped us find you. And we can't thank them enough."

"Did you know the woman who took her?" asked Knight.

"Adelaide was my cousin. She wanted a baby of her own so bad. It was very sad. Miscarriage after miscarriage. And no man in her life to speak of, not like my Harry." The woman reached out her hand for her husband.

"I'm sorry for your loss," said Knight. "Usually the first twenty-four hours in a missing child situation are critical. How did her disappearance play out? When did you know Lette was missing?"

"We went to a weekend revival meeting in Little Rock with our church. We're both in the choir. And Adelaide volunteered to watch Lette. I thought it would be a good thing, seeing how she'd just lost another baby. When we got back Sunday night they were gone."

Lette pulled at her mother's arm. "Can we go home now?"

"Yes, sweetheart." Lette's mother held out her hand, and Lette took it. "Let's all go home."

ACKNOWLEDGEMENTS

Two well-researched books sparked the fire that created Deception.

The first, *China RX* by Rosemary Gibson, opened my eyes to the pharmaceutical world and exposed me to information about where and how our medications are actually manufactured.

The second, *Bottle of Lies* by Katherine Eban, deepened my understanding of the process and how easy it was for America to lose control of our pharmaceutical supply. Both books are well worth your time to read.

And I have to admit, every time I get a new supply of my various medications, I do look at the pills and wish I had access to a mass spectrometer so I could be sure of their real chemical makeup.

THANK YOU...

No story can be written without the help and support of many wonderful people.

My muse, Carolyn Koppe, was again by my side as I drafted Deception, giving me advice and challenging me when I got stuck. I truly appreciate your time and energy and your belief in the story I wanted to tell.

Mish Kara one of my beta readers loved the story and told me she thought it was my best to date. Talk about encouragement!

My editor, Faith Freewoman, at Demon for Details, totally rocks! What a pleasure and honor it has been to work with you on this story. Your generosity of spirit gently guided my writing efforts, helped me smooth out plot lines and add depth to my characters.

Thank you Dar Dixon for a fantastic cover. You are a talented graphic designer and a joy to partner with. Thank you to Amy Atwell and your team at Author E.M.S. Your formatting skills are priceless.

John, your love and support is what every woman wants from her husband and what I consider myself so lucky to have. You are a blessing in my life.